IN DANGER

Australian praise for *The Minivers*:

*"Prior brings together great writing, highly imaginative
plots that positively rocket along and a freshness of
spirit that is terrifically appealing"*
KIDSPOT, Australia

*"Natalie Jane Prior has a deep understanding
of children and what they enjoy reading"*
JANUARY MAGAZINE, Australia

*"The adventures proceed at a cracking pace,
with kidnapping, escape in a delivery crate and a
scary scene at the funfair. All good nail-biting fun,
but a few serious lessons are learned"*
JUNIOR MAGAZINE, Australia

*"So exciting I couldn't put it down. I highly
recommend this book"*
TOWNSVILLE BULLETIN, Australia

MINIVERS STILL MISSING

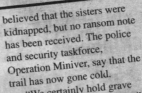

THREE WEEKS after their mysterious disappearance, authorities are no closer to explaining what has happened to Artemisia's celebrated Miniver sisters.

Emily and Rosamund Miniver, the foster daughters of Artemisia's ruler, Papa King, went missing from their home on the night of 6th October, shortly after a birthday party for Rosamund at the Artemisia Hotel ended with tears and an unexplained tantrum from the miniature star. At first it was

believed that the sisters were kidnapped, but no ransom note has been received. The police and security taskforce, Operation Miniver, say that the trail has now gone cold.

"We certainly hold grave fears for the Minivers' safety," said Minivers Security Chief, Ron Burton. "Operation Miniver would like to talk to anyone who thinks they have information. Our lines remain open, on 1001-MINIVER."

A palace spokeswoman, Miss Adelaide Clark, says that Papa King has not been told of the sisters' disappearance. Artemisia's ruler suffered a severe stroke eleven months ago, and it is believed that the shock would be too much for him. Papa King has been the sisters' foster father since Rosamund was found in a shoe box on the steps of the Royal Artemisia Hospital fourteen years ago.

SPENDING CUTS NOT TRUE, SAYS PALACE

PALACE financial administrator Len Smeaton has denied he is planning savage cuts to public spending.

Citizens have recently been alarmed by rumours of a nightly curfew in which all street lights would be turned off to save electricity. There has also been talk that all police cars will be replaced with second-hand vehicles, garbage services will be cut back to a once a month collection, and that all of Artemisia's twenty-seven public libraries will be closed.

"I know nothing about this at all," said Mr Smeaton, though he added that he had no problem with the idea of the library closures. "As far as I'm concerned, if people want books, they should pay for them," he said.

SERENA SIMPSON TO BUILD NEW MANSION

POPULAR TV INTERVIEWER, Serena Simpson, is planning to build a new mansion in the Artemisia Hills.

The ten-bedroom, five-bathroom mansion will feature an indoor squash court, a rooftop pool, and a soda fountain and hamburger bar for Serena's two sons. While Serena remains tight-lipped, security on her new home is expected to be state-of-the-art, as Artemisian celebrities continue to panic over the recent unsolved disappearance of pop sensations Rosamund and Emily Miniver.

Friends of Serena expressed surprise, as the blonde star was reputed to be having financial problems following a series of bad investments, and a bitter divorce from Artemisian tennis champion, Wally Stamper.

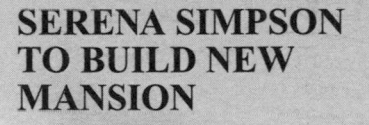

TRACY T HITS NUMBER ONE
Minivers Dethroned

"Sick Bunny", the new song by Tracy T, and her band the Vampire Girls, has knocked the Minivers' hit, "By My Side", off the top spot to debut in the Artemisia Top Ten at Number One.

Artemisia's Goth Girl is the first artist apart from the Miniver sisters to debut in the top chart position for seven years. "I think people are getting sick of the Minivers," said Tracy. "They want music with real bite."

"By My Side" was only at Number One for four weeks, making it the weakest selling Minivers song to date. A spokesman from Miniver Records refused to comment.

NO TRUTH IN FUNFAIR MINIVER SIGHTINGS

Reports that Emily Miniver was seen running from armed security guards at the Artemisian Funfair last weekend are unfounded, according to Minivers Security Chief, and Head of Operation Miniver, Ron Burton.

"I am afraid there is no truth in these stories," said Mr Burton.

"Operation Miniver has looked into the matter carefully, and it seems that a little girl who was visiting the funfair with her father and brother was chased through the grounds after escaping from her family. She was safely returned to them by funfair security staff."

Rumours that Emily Miniver was seen dangling from the funfair's Big Wheel was denied by the park's management.

The Minivers Crisis Line is still open for anyone wishing to report sightings of the missing sisters. The free-call number at Operation Miniver is 1001-MINIVER.

MADAME VOWS TO FIND MISSING SISTERS

Madame, daughter of Artemisia's ruler, Papa King, has vowed to find her missing foster sisters, the Minivers.

"Emily and Rosamund are like family to me," a tearful Madame told our reporter. "I would give anything to know where they are."

Madame, aged 31, has spent most of her adult life in mysterious exile. She returned to Artemisia shortly after Papa King's stroke, and has recently undergone a spectacular makeover. Our political commentators suggest that she may be preparing to take over from her ailing father as Queen of Artemisia.

Natalie Jane Prior was born in Brisbane, Australia, in November, 1963. Her father is English, and her mother Australian. As a child, she spent most of her time with her nose in a book, or writing doll-sized stories for her friends during maths lessons. She made up her mind to be a children's author when she was about ten, and although she worked for a while as a librarian for a gold-mining company, she has never seriously wanted to do anything else.

Natalie published her first book, *The Amazing Adventures of Amabel*, in 1990. Since then she has written picture books, prize-winning novels and even a best-selling book about mummies! Some of her other books include *The Paw* (illustrated by Terry Denton), a picture book about a cat burglar, and the *Lily Quench* series, which has been published in many countries around the world. Natalie started working on the *Minivers* because she wanted to write a book about what it's like to be on the run when you're only two feet tall and everyone knows what you look like.

Natalie lives in Brisbane with her husband and daughter and two miniature dachshunds called Rupert and Jasmine, in a house with a dragon on the roof.

the MINIVERS

IN DANGER

Natalie Jane Prior

mlb
MARION LLOYD BOOKS

First published in the UK in 2010 by Marion Lloyd Books
An imprint of Scholastic Children's Books
Euston House, 24 Eversholt Street
London, NW1 1DB, UK
A division of Scholastic Ltd.
Registered office: Westfield Road, Southam, Warwickshire, CV47 0RA
SCHOLASTIC and associated logos are trademarks and/
or registered trademarks of Scholastic Inc.

Copyright © Natalie Jane Prior, 2009
First published in Australia by Pearson Australia Group Pty Ltd, 2009
The right of Natalie Jane Prior to be identified as the author
of this work has been asserted by her.

ISBN 9781407110455

A CIP catalogue record for this book
is available from the British Library

Printed by CPI Bookmarque Ltd, Croydon, Surrey
Papers used by Scholastic Children's Books are made
from wood grown in sustainable forests.

3 5 7 9 10 8 6 4 2

This is a work of fiction. Names, characters, places, incidents and dialogues
are products of the author's imagination or are used fictitiously. Any resemblance
to actual people, living or dead, events or locales is entirely coincidental.

www.scholastic.co.uk/zone

For Ralph and Sylvia Bowles

1

FUGITIVES IN THE HILLS

Emily Miniver lay on a rock in the sunshine, looking out across the tops of the trees. It was a curious situation for her to be in. She was so very small and the sky above so very big. The forest in front of her seemed to stretch on without finish. Emily had never before been anywhere she could not see buildings. For the first time in her entire famous life, she felt insignificant.

The rock under her tummy was warm from the sun. Emily was sweaty and dishevelled from climbing, but in a funny way she felt good about it. Her clothes were dirty, her once glossy dark hair was dull from lack of washing, and her perfectly manicured nails were torn and broken. Emily even suspected she was smelly, but after three weeks on the run she was surprised to find how little these things mattered. She was simply glad to be free.

A lizard scuttled over the rock. Birds flew overhead and Emily shaded her eyes and looked up at them, wondering what they were. The only birds she had known before coming to the forest were city crows and sparrows, and the ducks in the palace ponds back in Artemisia. Emily screwed up her eyes and tried to focus on something flying low over the trees in the far distance, but the sun dazzled her, and before she was able to work out what it was, she was distracted by a shout from below.

"Emmie?"

Emily sat up. Her older sister, Rosamund, was picking her way doggedly through the scrub in the gully below, her two-foot high figure looking tiny against the trees, holding up the hem of the oversized T-shirt she was wearing as a sort of dress. She looked very different from the Rosamund of a few weeks before, who had been the miniature idol of the Artemisian pop charts, and the beloved foster daughter of Papa King, Artemisia's ruler. *That* Rosamund would never have been seen in public without make-up, designer clothes and an escort of security guards all three times her own diminutive size. Now, even Rosamund's long black hair had been cut short like a boy's in an attempt to disguise her identity, and her face, which had looked confident and in control, was drawn and worried. Feeling slightly guilty, Emily went running down to meet her.

"There you are!" said Rosamund, when Emily reached the gully. "What on earth were you doing up there alone? You know Gibraltar told us not to go off by ourselves."

"I'm sorry, Rose." Emily tried hard to sound as if she meant it, but Rosamund wasn't fooled. In the days when they had been celebrities and the stars of their own TV show, they had gone to the same drama teacher.

"You're not sorry at all," said Rosamund. "You were positively enjoying yourself. Emmie, don't you realize being here's dangerous for people as tiny as us? It's bad enough having to sleep in that cave, without you falling down a cliff, or being eaten by wild animals—"

"What wild animals?" Emily burst out laughing. "Come on, Rose. There's nothing here but foxes, and they only come out at night. As for falling, I wasn't anywhere near the edge. I was perfectly safe." As she spoke, a noise in the background, which until now she had scarcely noticed, started growing unexpectedly louder. It silenced the creaks and rustles of the trees, the soft call of the birds, and the gurgle of the creek flowing through the gully. Emily looked up. She knew this sound, had heard it a thousand times before, but in this quiet setting it was so completely out of place she could not at first work out what it was.

"What's that?" Rosamund lifted her eyes in panic. At

that moment, belated recognition punched through Emily's confusion.

"Quick!" she shouted. "Run! Back to the cave!"

Emily seized Rosamund's hand and dived into the nearest bit of scrub, dragging her sister after her. Rosamund too, had recognized the sound now for what it was. It was a helicopter, approaching very low, and its driving, mechanical beat cut through the air and sent vibrations shuddering over the rocks. The trees bent their branches over the Minivers' heads. Their dark hair ruffled wildly about their faces and they were surrounded by a stinging whirlwind of leaves and earth.

"It's too far!" Rosamund yelled. "We'll never make it back. Quick, follow me!" She dragged her hand out of Emily's and started leaping across the wet rocks to the other side of the creek. Emily followed, her trainered feet splashing and plunging in the shallow water. On the last rock she lost her footing and fell, only to be caught by Rosamund and pulled on to the muddy bank. Dripping and panting, the two girls crammed into a hole in a hollow tree trunk and cowered inside.

The helicopter was lowering over the creek. It hovered for what seemed like for ever, ruffling the surface of the water and sending fine droplets spraying like rain over the creek banks. The noise of its engine was deafening. Emily felt the wind from the rotors on her dripping legs and buried her face in Rosamund's shoulder. Rosamund put her arms around her and squeezed her own eyes tight shut.

"Oh, no," she whispered. "Not again!"

The Minivers shrank against the rough inside of the trunk. A splinter dug into Emily's arm and she bit her lip to stop from crying out. Then the beat of the rotors changed its note. There was a flash of metal in the sunlight, the stink of exhaust fumes, and the helicopter headed up the creek and flew away.

Several minutes passed before Emily and Rosamund dared stir inside the hollow tree. At first they simply stood, holding on to each other, both lost in terrible memories. Rosamund remembered her disastrous birthday party on the last night of their old life, an evening that had ended with her being dragged from her bed by kidnappers. Emily thought of the terrifying week she had spent on the run, and of the sinister Vice-President of the Minivers Fan Club, Titus, who had hunted her and almost caught her. Both of them thought of Madame. It was Papa King's daughter Karen, known as Madame, who had turned against the Minivers and tried to destroy them. She had driven them from their home and imprisoned their beloved housekeeper, Millamant. The helicopter did not need to have Madame's name written on it. There was simply no one else who could have sent it.

"Is it safe to go outside yet?" whispered Rosamund.

Emily listened intently. The helicopter had gone, but it seemed to her that they were not alone. She could sense, rather than hear, the sound of footsteps, crunching on the gravel down near the water. Rosamund whimpered, and pressed her hand quickly over her mouth. The footsteps grew louder and closer until there was no mistaking them. Finally they reached the tree and stopped.

"Rosamund? Emily?"

At the sound of the familiar voice, Rosamund let out an inadvertent shriek. There was a brief tangle as both girls tried to bolt through the narrow entrance at the same time, and then Emily shot out into the sunlight. Rosamund tumbled after her and the two of them landed in an undignified heap at the feet of a tall swarthy man. He was dressed in torn jeans, a khaki shirt and heavy hiking boots, and carried a backpack. It was their friend Gibraltar, who had helped them escape from Artemisia and found them their hiding place in the forest.

Rosamund picked herself up and flung herself at Gibraltar's legs. "Gibraltar! What are you doing here? We weren't expecting you back until next week!"

"There's been a change of plan," said Gibraltar. "I'm not here with supplies this time. I'm here to take you away, and not a moment too soon, from the look of that helicopter. If it had landed, neither of you would have stood a chance." He pointed to the muddy ground, where dozens of miniature footprints led straight to the tree where they had been hiding.

"Oops," said Rosamund. Emily looked shamefaced, but Gibraltar only smiled.

"No harm done," he said. "But there's lots to tell you, and that helicopter's still searching. Let's get back to the cave as quickly as we can."

The cave where Emily and Rosamund had been camping was only a short distance uphill. Gibraltar, who seemed to know the whole area very well, had chosen it for them because it was close to water, and because it had more than one exit in case of emergency. He led the way swiftly through the trees, and the Minivers had to hurry on their short legs to keep pace.

"What's been happening?" Emily asked.

"Things are changing in Artemisia," said Gibraltar. "I don't know what it is, but there's definitely something brewing. The search for you has spread beyond the city, so you can't hide here any longer. But there's something else happening, too. In the last few days, all Minivers products have vanished out of the shops. Minivers advertising has disappeared, your TV show's off air and Radio Artemisia has stopped playing your music. You're not even in the news any more. It's as if the two of you have suddenly ceased to exist."

Emily and Rosamund stopped in their tracks and stared at him.

"What do you mean?" said Rosamund. "That's impossible. Emily and I are the Minivers. Everybody in Artemisia knows us. We're famous."

"No, Rose," said Gibraltar. "What I'm trying to tell you is that you *were* famous."

An unpleasant silence followed this remark. Emily glanced at Rosamund's face and thought she looked as if somebody she knew had just died.

"I don't understand," said Rosamund, in a small flat voice.

"Neither do I," said Gibraltar. "But I fully intend to, and that's why I've come to take you back."

The three of them started walking again, Emily and Rosamund now silent and thoughtful. In about a minute, they reached the cave and slipped under the overhanging rock that hid the entrance.

Inside was a small, round space, filled with sleeping

bags, storm lanterns and camping gear. Gibraltar and their other friend, Livia Wallace, had done their best to set things up as comfortably as possible, but it was still far rougher than anything they had known before. Rosamund looked around. She had not been happy here, yet she felt strangely reluctant at the thought of leaving. Night after night she had lain in her oversized sleeping bag, poring over Minivers articles in the old magazines Livia gave them and crying about everything they had lost. Rosamund had told herself that it was all a huge mistake; that sooner or later someone, somewhere, would put things right so she could go home. Now the longed-for moment had come, but it was not the return she had wanted. What was the point of going back if she could not be famous? If she was not to be Rosamund Miniver, the celebrity almost-princess, then who on earth was she to become?

"Pack your things up quickly," said Gibraltar. "We don't have a lot of time. I've arranged for Livia to meet us with her car on the old Artemisia Road at seven tonight. It's a long walk, so only take what you absolutely need."

Reluctantly, Rosamund started gathering up her possessions. She filled her water bottle, found her hat, and helped Gibraltar hide the camping gear behind some boulders at the back of the cave. Emily put on her backpack and went to wait by the entrance. She stood for a moment, looking down the hill towards the creek. It seemed to her that something was moving among the trees and she squinted, trying to make out what it was. A flash of light blue, the colour of the sky. . .

"Gibraltar!" Emily shot back into the cave. "There are Minivers security people down in the gully. They must have come in the helicopter!"

"Our footprints! They'll see them!" Rosamund started running for the entrance. Gibraltar grabbed her by the shoulder.

"Not that way. Out the back." Gibraltar hustled both girls towards the darkest part of the cave. "Remember, they can't know for certain that we're here. Keep calm and quiet, and do exactly as I say. Everything will be all right."

He pushed Emily and Rosamund into a narrow crack in the back wall of the cave. They emerged into pitch darkness. Emily stretched out her hands and felt nothing in front of her; she turned back, but could not find Rosamund either. Then a torch switched on and she saw her sister's face illuminated palely by its wan light. Gibraltar was squeezing through the gap behind her, blocking the light and air from the cave behind.

"Straight up," he said, nodding, and Emily saw that

there was a sort of slope before her, covered with earth and gravel. She started to climb, feeling, rather than seeing, where she was headed, and ignoring Rosamund's complaints as the gravel showered down. After a minute or two, the slope narrowed to a shaft like a chimney and she came to a halt.

"I'm stuck!"

"It's not far now." Gibraltar came up behind her and gave her a boost. Emily reached up. Her arms snagged in what felt like a tangle of roots, and she grabbed them and started to wriggle upwards. Earth showered down on her face and she coughed and screwed up her eyes. Gibraltar gave one last shove from underneath and she popped up into a clump of bushes like a rabbit out of a hole.

Emily rolled aside quickly to make room for Rosamund, and then Gibraltar. The three of them crouched in the bushes, looking down the hill in the direction of the creek. A line of men in blue Miniver House security uniforms was moving stealthily up the slope towards the cave. Emily bit her lip at the sight of the familiar faces. She glanced at Rosamund and saw that her expression was grim.

"Come on," whispered Gibraltar. "There's nothing we can do here."

He slipped into the trees and Rosamund followed

obediently. As she stood up, Emily paused and looked out across the treetops. On the other side of the creek she could see the rock where she had lain and thought she was free. It had been a marvellous feeling. Emily could not help wondering if she would ever know it again.

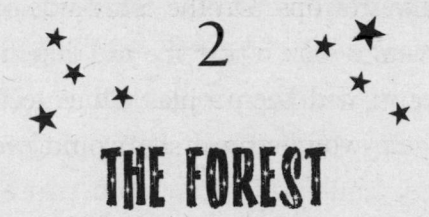

2

THE FOREST

Gibraltar headed uphill, away from the gully where the searchers had first been sighted, keeping to the thickest part of the forest. Emily and Rosamund carried their belongings in toddler-sized backpacks, slung over their shoulders. The packs were not particularly heavy but the going was rough. Since their tiny legs had to work three times as hard as Gibraltar's, it was not long before they were panting from the effort.

Bushes that came up to Gibraltar's knees threatened to engulf them. Rocks he could easily step over had to be climbed or walked around. Gibraltar tried to choose the smoothest path, but as the ground grew steeper and the trees thicker, it was not always easy for him to do this. Often he had to stop and wait for Emily and Rosamund to catch up. Once or twice he even had to carry them, and though they both normally hated being treated like babies, for once neither girl protested.

The helicopter could still be heard, sweeping over the trees. It was further off now, but it was obvious that it was following a search pattern, and that the pilot was communicating with the people on the ground. On the second hill, they stopped briefly for Gibraltar to consult his compass. Emily and Rosamund paused to catch their breath and swigged greedily from their water bottles.

"Do you think they're following us?" Emily asked.

"That depends," Gibraltar replied. "I didn't see any dogs, but if the guards have them, they'll already be on our trail."

"Dogs?" Rosamund's face went a trifle paler. At Miniver House the guards patrolled at night with trained Dobermanns. They were taller than she was, and even on leashes she had always found them terrifying. "Do you mean, guard dogs?"

"Bloodhounds," said Gibraltar. "Tracker animals, trained to find missing people, or bring down criminals. If they have them, they'll have picked up our scent at the cave. There's also the chance that we might meet another search party coming in the opposite direction. In either case, there's nothing we can do. Our best hope of escape is to keep moving as quickly as possible."

Rosamund and Emily stopped asking questions.

They put away their water bottles and followed Gibraltar to the top of the hill, where he struck out along a ridge that swung away to the west. The ground continued to climb slowly, and the forest grew so dense they lost all sense of direction. If she had felt small on the rock above the creek, thought Emily, she and Rosamund might as well have been insects here. The trees were taller and greener, and their canopies were so intertwined that they blotted out the sunlight. Some had fluted trunks that thrust out into the earth like the fins on a rocket. Others were ancient giants with gnarled curtains of trailing roots. It was cooler and quieter, though from time to time the bell-like calls of birds and the sound of running water echoed eerily through the stillness. Mosquitoes buzzed. Bracket fungi grew from fallen tree trunks, and there was a smell of leaf litter, mud and decay.

Finally, Gibraltar called a halt. The Minivers were so tired that they dropped their bags and almost collapsed where they stood.

"Here. Have something to eat." Gibraltar opened his backpack and brought out some biscuits and fruit. Emily sat down on a fallen log and ate several cheese crackers and a handful of sultanas. Rosamund devoured an apple. As they ate, they slapped at the mosquitoes hovering around them. Their arms and legs were already covered in bites and scratches from fighting through the undergrowth.

"As soon as I get back to Artemisia," said Rosamund, tossing away her apple core, "I'm going to have a proper meal. Grilled steak and mashed potatoes, with tomato and green peas. I want a bath, too. I'm fed up with washing in creeks and puddles."

"Don't get too hopeful. We've a long way to go yet," said Gibraltar. He looked around uneasily and checked his watch. "Come on. We'd better get moving again. It'll be dark in an hour or two and we have to reach the road before nightfall."

Rosamund's face fell. "Already?" she protested. "Can't we rest? I'm *so* tired. Five minutes now isn't going to make any difference later."

"The longer you stop, the harder it will be to get going again," said Gibraltar, but at the sight of Emily's white, exhausted face, he relented. "All right. Ten minutes' rest, but no more. Wait here while I scout ahead."

"Why is he so worried?" demanded Rosamund, as Gibraltar disappeared into the trees. "There's no one around. We're perfectly safe."

"I hope so." Emily shivered. The trees were so thick, it was impossible to see more than a few dozen paces in any direction. "I just wish we knew more about what's happening in Artemisia. Who knows what we're going to find when we get back? And what about Milly and Fiona? When I think about how we ran away and left them behind, I feel so ashamed."

"We didn't have any choice, Emmie," said Rosamund. She understood perfectly why Emily was so worried. Fiona was one of their fans, a girl Emily's age who had risked everything to help them, while Millamant, their old housekeeper, was like family. "Madame was after us. If we'd stayed any longer, we'd have been caught. Anyway, we do know where Milly is. Livia told us she was locked up in the Bridge House."

"She *was* locked up there," said Emily miserably. "That was two weeks ago. By now she could be anywhere, and Fiona, too."

Since Rosamund knew this was right, the conversation died. The Minivers sat together in silence, their ears strained for the sound of Gibraltar's return. Rosamund's thoughts strayed to what lay ahead. It occurred to her that in going home they were merely leaving the forest for a different kind of wilderness. Their old friends and their old lives were all gone. And even if they discovered what mischief Madame was up to, they were powerless to stop her. Rosamund glanced over at Emily. She was still brooding, no doubt about Millamant. The fact made Rosamund uneasy, though she did not know why.

At last Gibraltar re-emerged from the trees.

"There's a creek ahead," he reported. "We're going to have to ford it, but it's not impossible. On your feet, now. We can't afford to hang around any longer."

Rosamund had grown cold sitting on the damp log, so she did not mind moving on quite as much as she had expected. She and Emily picked up their backpacks, and the three of them set off. Soon after they left the clearing, the ground began to slope away in front of them and the going became more difficult. Emily and Rosamund found themselves slipping in the mud, and clutched at vines and bushes to stop themselves from falling. The sound of rushing water could be heard somewhere below. They slithered down a steep slope, half on their bottoms, and emerged on the rocky banks of a swift-flowing creek.

Gibraltar knelt and showed them his compass. "We have to cross here," he said. "The road's due south on the other side. It doesn't look too deep, but the water's fast and it might be slippery, so it will be best if I carry you. Wait here, and I'll work out the best place to cross."

Gibraltar stepped from rock to rock, looking for the safest way over the creek. Emily waited until Gibraltar was halfway over, then waded in a few steps after him.

Her tiny legs sank deep into the water, and she gave a yelp of shock at the cold.

"It's *freezing*!" The water churned around Emily's hips and her teeth chattered. Rosamund hesitated on the bank, her oversized T-shirt held above her knees. She glanced down at her legs and saw that they were dotted with bits of mud from her slide down the slope. Rosamund bent down to brush them off, but they clung to her skin and would not shift. Finally a piece dropped off and a tiny trickle of blood ran down her calf. Rosamund stared in revolted disbelief and gave an ear-splitting shriek.

"*Leeches!* Help, I've got *leeches!*"

Gibraltar turned in the middle of the creek. He was too far away to do anything, but Emily immediately waded back a few paces and tried to pick the leeches off. Rosamund screamed again.

"Don't touch me!"

"Rose, keep still, I'm trying to help!" A blood-filled leech squished messily between Emily's fingers. The sight of its swollen body bursting was more than Rosamund could stand, and as Emily reached for the next one she kicked out violently at her sister's hand. Emily dodged, but she was standing on slippery rocks and her footing was precarious. Her arms flew up, her feet went out from under her, and she lost her

19

balance and fell with a smacking thud against a nearby rock.

"Emily!" Gibraltar sprang towards the bank, but it was too late. Emily hit the water with a splash. A small hand flailed up above the surface, and then the fast-moving current swept her into the deepest part of the creek and bore her away.

"Wait!" Rosamund saw Gibraltar diving into the water, and jumped after him without hesitation. She was a good swimmer, but the fast-flowing creek was nothing like the Miniver House swimming pool, and she realized immediately that she had made a mistake. The current was so powerful there was no way she could swim, or even grab hold of the rocks that were swirling past. Her arms and legs scraped and banged against them, and the backpack she was wearing weighed her down. Rosamund struggled against its straps and swallowed mouthfuls of freezing water. The current was dragging her under, and there was nothing she could do to keep from drowning.

"Help!" Rosamund gurgled. "Help!" Suddenly a rock loomed up in front of her. She smashed painfully into it and tried to grab hold. In that instant a large hand grasped her wrist and yanked her to a stop.

"If you want to avoid going back home," said Gibraltar, "you're going the right way about it."

He dragged Rosamund to the opposite bank and pushed her up on to the rocks. Rosamund sprawled limply, coughing up water. Her teeth were chattering so hard she thought they would break, but it did not matter. Gibraltar was carrying Emily under his other arm. Her eyes were dazed and there was a bloody graze on her forehead, but she was conscious and alive. It was, Rosamund realized, far more than she deserved. Whatever awaited the two of them in Artemisia, it could not be worse than arriving there alone.

At the back of an unkempt garden in Woodside, Artemisia, stood a shabby green aluminium shed. It was full of garden tools and fertilizers, and since its owner was not very fond of gardening it was rarely visited. Recently, however, the shed had been put to another purpose. An unseen prisoner was kicking frantically against its metal walls, and the sound of her sobs and shouts floated up the path to the house where the Minivers Fan Club Committee was meeting.

"Let me out! Please! Let me *out*!"

A young man with unkempt blond hair was sitting with his trainered feet on Brenda Bertram's kitchen table. It was Titus, the club's Vice-President, and head of the mysterious organization known as Operation Miniver. The sound of the prisoner's screams seemed to amuse him, and he cocked his head in their direction.

"Our Fiona's certainly got a good set of lungs," he remarked.

Holly, who liked to think of herself as Titus's girlfriend, looked out of the window and scowled. "I wish she'd shut up."

"Yes," put in Len, the club's treasurer. "If somebody hears her, we could be in awful trouble." Ron Burton, the Minivers' former Chief of Security, said nothing, but the newest member of the committee looked scared, and winced. Brenda Bertram was Fiona's mother. In a dim corner of her brain, she had an idea that the police did not approve of parents who locked their children up in tool sheds. Unfortunately for Fiona, Brenda was too afraid of Titus and Holly to say so.

"You're right, Len. We've heard enough," said Titus with a sigh. He took his feet off the table. "Go and let Fiona out, Holly. She's been a very naughty girl."

Holly hopped up and disappeared down the back steps. Titus watched from the window until she reached the shed, then flicked the curtain closed and smiled at Brenda. A minute or two later, the flyscreen door banged open and Holly reappeared, dragging with her a sturdy girl with brown eyes and a tear-stained, freckled face.

Fiona Bertram had been on the run for nearly a fortnight. She had helped Emily and Rosamund Miniver escape from the Artemisia Funfair on the very night when Titus had planned their capture, and then she herself had fled. After ten days of sleeping under bridges and eating out of rubbish bins, her hair was matted and her clothes were filthy. Yet even now, after being locked up in the shed on bread and water, a hint of defiance lingered in her eyes. Though Holly forced her to sit down in the chair opposite Titus, Fiona could not stop herself struggling.

For a moment there was silence. Holly stood beside Fiona's chair, ready to shove her back into it if necessary, while Brenda went white and pressed her hands together. Fiona glared at Titus and tried to hold on to a mental picture of Emily Miniver. Emily had outwitted Titus, not once, but three times. If she could do it, so could Fiona. But then, Emily had not been locked up in the shed. It had been hot in there, dark and airless, and it stank of chemicals and mower fuel. Fiona had hoped vainly that her mother might come to free her, but Brenda had never been able to stand up to Titus. The dreadful fear Fiona had been pushing down for days welled up again inside her. Under Titus's stern gaze, the image of Emily Miniver, so brave and tiny and tough, slowly faded from her mind.

"You've been a very naughty girl, Fiona," said Titus mildly. "You've given us all a lot of trouble. But I've got some good news for you. We're going to give you another chance."

Fiona tried to meet Titus's eyes, but his expression was too dreadful, and she could not do it. Holly's fingers dug into her neck and she trembled in her chair. Titus waited a moment, then continued.

"All I want from you is information. I need to know where you met the Minivers, who is helping them and what they're planning."

Fiona looked at her lap. Titus spoke again, even more softly than before.

"So. It's to be like that, is it, Fiona? Think very carefully. I can always send you back to the shed." Fiona glanced up, and Titus caught the flicker of fear in her eyes. "Perhaps . . . with just water this time? I know how hard it is for a growing girl to go hungry, but" – he shrugged expressively – "you're not really giving us very much choice, are you?"

Holly picked up a piece of squashy bun from a plate on the table. She pulled it apart and ate the pieces, bit by bit. Brenda swallowed and pressed her hands into a tight little ball.

"Emily Miniver is my friend," said Fiona. She lifted her eyes and fastened them steadily on Titus. "*My friend.* I'm glad I helped her escape. I'd do it all over again, if I had the chance —" Fiona stopped. The expression in Titus's eyes had just crossed into his whole face.

"Thank you, Fiona," said Titus evenly. "I'm glad you feel Emily is your friend. From my own point of view, however, you are becoming a great nuisance. There is a place where nuisances are sent and I am going to send you there now. Maybe, when you've had time to think things over, you might change your mind. Holly — deal with it."

Holly dusted her sticky hands on her jeans and grabbed Fiona by the collar. Fiona screamed and struggled, but Holly was strong. She yanked Fiona off the chair and on to her feet. Fiona kicked and fought back, biting and scratching at Holly's arm. A chair tipped over. Fiona grabbed the table and held on with all her might.

"Mummy!" she screamed. "Mummy, *help me!*"

Brenda looked away. Tears were pouring down her cheeks, and she reached for her handkerchief. "Oh dear," she whispered brokenly. "Oh, dear."

Holly grabbed Fiona's wrist and prised her fingers free from the tabletop. Len looked rather ill, and Ron, whose own son Alex was about Fiona's age, stared out of the window. Titus listened impassively while Fiona was carried out the door and down the stairs to Holly's car. For a moment, his eyes rested on Brenda, and then he nodded and addressed the committee.

"Any objections?" There was no reply. "Good," said Titus. "Then let's get on with Phase Two."

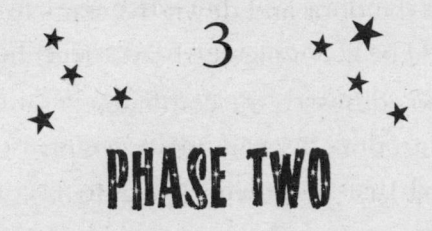

3

PHASE TWO

At the TV-6 studio on Miniver Boulevard, Madame sat staring disconsolately into a make-up mirror. The face reflected there looked very different to the one she was used to. Her wispy hair had been cut in a smart new fringe and her pale skin was smeared with make-up that hid the worst of her freckles. But Madame was not a fool. She knew that the person in the mirror did not look like a TV star or, for that matter, the future queen of Artemisia. In fact, if she had passed herself in the street, she would never have given herself a second glance.

Madame fingered the ruffled collar of her white silk dress. It was very similar to one she had seen Rosamund wear in the last-ever episode of *The Minivers' Music Hour*, but though it was extremely pretty, she could not help fretting about how much it had cost. Madame winced, thinking of the other new dresses, shoes and handbags she had been obliged to buy. It was terrible, the expense of being famous. Well, Titus and the others might insist she spend the money now, but when she became queen, things would be very different. Madame let her thoughts drift over the wonderful cost-cutting measures she was going to introduce as part of her reforms. Then she remembered that in order for her to become queen, certain documents hidden in the Most Secret Room must be found and destroyed. Madame wondered how much longer it was going to take her cousin Livia, who worked in the City Archives, to find them. Of late, Livia's behaviour had been very strange. . . Something like suspicion trembled in the back of Madame's mind, but before she could pursue her thoughts any further, the door opened and Titus came in.

Madame scowled at him. "Knock first, can't you?"

Titus merely smiled at her. He sat down on a plastic chair, crossed his long legs in their shabby jeans, and stretched comfortably. The door opened a second time, and Len entered, carrying a large rectangular parcel. Madame looked at it suspiciously.

"What's that?"

Len coughed. "It's the presentation cheque for Ron's son, Alex Burton. Ron was promised $100,000 for his role in Operation Miniver, remember?"

Madame shuddered. "That awful little boy."

"He's not an awful little boy," Titus rebuked her. "He

is a poor crippled child, who's been very badly treated by those selfish Miniver sisters. And *you* are going to help him."

"But I don't *want* to help him," said Madame. "Why should I? I couldn't care less if he's in a wheelchair—"

She stopped abruptly. Titus had fixed her eyes sternly with his own pale blue ones. "He is a poor crippled child," he repeated, "and you are going to help him, out of the kindness of your heart. That is what I have planned. Phase Two is ready to begin: don't spoil it. Play your part, like a good girl, and you will get to be queen. That's what you want, isn't it?"

Madame opened her mouth. She was saved from the embarrassment of having nothing to say by the arrival of a production assistant.

"The Burtons are with Serena now, Madame. We're about to go on air. Will you come with me?"

Trying hard to look like a queen, Madame swept out of the room.

The assistant led her down a rabbit-warren of badly lit passages to the main studio. Inside, the set was full of light and shadows, bustle and movement. Madame had appeared on TV quite a lot recently, and was getting used to the organized chaos that went on behind the scenes, but she secretly still found it all rather a thrill. Was this how it had been on *The Minivers' Music Hour*?

Madame took her place, and then the assistant director was beside her, hastily explaining her cue, the production assistant was counting down time, and the On Air light glowed like a red eye on the wall. The music blared, the camera swung around on its boom and suddenly *The Serena Simpson Show* was on air.

Ron Burton and his wife, Sandra, were sitting on a leather sofa opposite Serena Simpson. Their son, Alex, was in his wheelchair beside them, looking uncomfortable and sullen. Serena Simpson was one of the most popular interviewers on Artemisian TV. She was dressed tonight in a green linen suit with pearls around her neck, and every blonde hair was glued in place. Fascinated, Madame watched as Serena smiled up at the camera and began her introduction, unconsciously copying each tilt of her famous head.

"Good evening, Artemisia," said Serena. "Tonight, a story that will shock and surprise you. Since the startling disappearance of Rosamund and Emily Miniver three weeks ago, news reports have concentrated on the mystery of what has happened to Artemisia's celebrity sisters. Now, for the first time, we learn of the Minivers' dark side. With Miniver House empty, stories of unbelievable extravagance are emerging. This evening, we bring you a guest who has first-hand experience of the Minivers' selfishness. For many years, Ron Burton was the Miniver sisters' Chief of Security. He's here now, with his wife Sandra, and eleven-year-old son, Alex.

"So let me get this straight, Ron," said Serena. "Two years ago, Alex was run over while riding his bicycle and nearly killed. It was a hit-and-run accident, wasn't it?"

"That's right," Ron nodded. "The police were never able to trace the car. We only know it was red because of the paint scrapes on Alex's bike."

Serena continued. "Alex crushed his hip and broke several other bones. He was in hospital for months following the accident, and since then he's been in a wheelchair. Sandra, is there any hope that Alex might one day walk again?"

Sandra's eyes welled with tears. "Not really," she said. "The doctors say he needs a big operation by the time he's twelve, but Ron and I haven't got the money."

"So if Alex doesn't have an operation in the next year, he'll be in a wheelchair for life?"

"Yes."

"And your husband has worked for the Minivers for how long?"

"Nine years," said Ron.

"Nine *years*? And the Minivers never even thought to offer help? Did they know about Alex's disability?"

"Of course they did—"

"They sent me presents when I was in the hospital,"

put in Alex suddenly. "I got a really neat radio-controlled car."

"Tragic," said Serena loudly. The camera hastily swung away from Alex. Watching on the monitors, Madame was impressed to see a real tear glistening in Serena's eye. "This poor child was the victim of a hit-and-run accident, and those heartless girls sent him a toy *car*."

"It was a good car," said Alex. "I really liked it."

"And the Minivers never once offered to pay for the operation that would help Alex walk?"

"No, never," said Ron, and his face, under the studio lights, was suddenly angry. "I don't think it even occurred to them. What's a hundred thousand dollars to them? Why, they'd spend that in a year on their clothes. If you only knew what they had in that house of theirs, you'd be sick. They're selfish, through and through. There's not a jot of feeling in them for anyone but themselves."

"Well, it certainly seems the Minivers are not the nice young girls we all thought them to be," said Serena. "And I'm sure our viewers will be interested in our special documentary report, *Inside Miniver House*, coming up next on TV-6. But in the meantime, I have some good news for Alex and his parents. Someone else with a kind heart wants to help them, even if the

Minivers don't, and she's here in this studio tonight. On behalf of the Palace, I'd like to welcome to *The Serena Simpson Show* an important royal guest . . . Madame."

Madame tripped forward on her unfamiliar high heels, the giant cheque under her arm. The bright studio lights blazed around her, and she smiled at the cameras and lifted a manicured hand. She felt like a saint, surrounded by a halo of heavenly light. This, after all, was what it was all about: being the centre of everyone's attention. Serena Simpson stood up to welcome her on to the set. She took Madame's hand in her firm clasp, and Madame bowed graciously and fixed her expression into a smile.

"Alex," she said, as the teleprompter rolled, "I'd like to present you with this cheque, as a mark of my concern for all the disabled citizens of Artemisia. . ." (For a moment, Madame felt a flicker of concern: would this mean *all* disabled Artemisians would want cheques from her? She certainly hoped not.) "I hope you will soon be able to run about and, er, play as well as other boys." Reluctantly, she took the cheque out from under her arm and handed it to Alex. It was so big he all but disappeared behind it. For a moment the camera lingered on the happy family in close-up, then it pulled back and Serena said, "Next, our specially commissioned documentary, *Inside Miniver House*. Have you ever wondered what goes on behind the pink-and-white walls of the Minivers' home? Stay tuned to TV-6 for our startling revelations. And now from me, Serena Simpson, good night."

The *Serena Simpson* theme began to play. As the camera swung away, an unseemly fight broke out on the set. Madame's instincts had got the better of her, and she was struggling to take back the cheque.

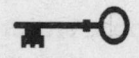

Livia Wallace sat in her parked car on the Artemisia Road, counting the minutes. The clock said it was eight-thirty, but she felt as if she had been waiting for ever. To her left was a tall stone cairn erected to the memory of some long-dead explorer. Livia could not remember his name, nor could she read in the dark what had happened to him, but she knew that he had been killed on this very mountain. The fact made it extremely hard to push back the fears that crowded inside her head.

It was not the first time that Livia had felt like this. Ever since she had found Rosamund hiding in the City Archives where she worked, she had been trying to help the Minivers, but it was getting harder and harder to keep doing this. Livia was a kind person, and she knew

Emily and Rosamund were being treated badly. On the other hand, Livia's cousin was Madame. Though she did not like her much, Livia hated having to tell her lies all the time, and the constant secrecy about the Minivers' whereabouts was making her so stressed she was becoming sick. Livia did not know how much longer she could go on.

A small glimmer appeared along the road a little way ahead. It was too dim to be a headlamp, but it was about the right size for a torch, and a moment later it was joined by a second light that looked as if it were being carried by someone very short. Relieved, Livia jumped out of her car and started hurrying towards the approaching lights. A moment later, she saw Rosamund, and Gibraltar carrying Emily on his shoulders, coming along the road towards her.

"Thank goodness you made it! I was starting to think—" Livia broke off, staring at the Minivers. Both girls were wet and filthy, covered with bloodied scratches and smears of mud. It was hard to believe these bedraggled creatures had once been so famous that people all over Artemisia had queued and fought to see them. They looked like tiny hunted animals.

Livia took Rosamund's sodden backpack from her and carried it to the car. She opened the boot and dropped it inside. Gibraltar set Emily down on the ground. She wobbled on her feet, and when Livia opened the door she collapsed on the back seat in an exhausted heap.

Livia started the car quickly and they headed off in the direction of Artemisia. As soon as they were under way, Emily snuggled up under a knitted blanket and tried to sleep. It was not easy, for the car had a noisy engine and her head was aching fiercely from the blow she'd received when she hit the rock. In between dozes, she heard snatches of conversation between Livia and Gibraltar: how Livia had seen the helicopter, hovering over the mountainside, and how Gibraltar had brought them safely through the last of the forest. Rosamund sat beside her with her hands in her lap, uncharacteristically quiet and reflective. From time to time she stroked Emily's hair, and the gentleness of the gesture and the swaying of the car sent Emily drifting at last into a troubled sleep.

Around ten o'clock, the car reached the outskirts of the city and slowed as it ran into unexpected traffic. Emily stirred, and sat up.

"What's happening?" she asked groggily.

"There's a traffic jam," said Rosamund. "I think there must be a fire somewhere. Can you smell the smoke?"

"Yes." Emily looked out of the window. Drifts of smoke were floating towards them, and she wrinkled her nose at the faint acrid smell. "Has there been an accident?"

"I don't think so." Livia peered through the windscreen, but while something was clearly going on up ahead of them, there was no sign of a crash. The car slowed almost to a crawl. A little further along they saw a smashed set of traffic lights and several shops with broken windows. Bits of brick and rubble were scattered over the footpath and the smoke grew thicker and more pungent.

"Wind the windows up," said Gibraltar suddenly, and his voice was such that they all obeyed without question. Livia turned the corner and they saw an orange glow ahead. Emily and Rosamund sat up in the back seat. A huge bonfire was burning in the middle of the street in front of them and scenes of rioting met their eyes. Gangs of youths were milling about, throwing bricks at windows and jumping on car bonnets. One car had been pushed on to the footpath and was being rocked back and forth with its driver still in it. Black oily smoke poured from the bonfire. It smelled of burning plastic. Unable to stop herself, Emily sat up to her full height and stared in horror at the hundreds of tiny corpses melting on the bonfire. They were life-sized Miniver dolls. She and Rosamund were being burned.

"*Get down!*" snapped Gibraltar, and Emily instantly

obeyed. She grabbed the knitted blanket and pulled it over Rosamund and herself. Rosamund's arms reached for her, and Emily felt both their hearts beating so quickly that she was sure they must be loud enough to hear. The car crept forward a few more lengths and came to a halt again. A teenage boy started walking towards them. In the driver's seat, Livia gave a muffled cry of alarm.

"Keep calm now, Livia," said Gibraltar, but Livia shook her head. She too, had seen the burning Miniver dolls, and she had also seen that the car being attacked had a distinctive Minivers sticker on the bumper. Livia's fingers turned white where they gripped the steering wheel. Her stomach churned until she thought she was going to be sick.

The boy swaggered up to the driver's window and banged on it. "Hey. You." Livia stared ahead and tried to ignore him, but he only banged harder. "You. Lady. Are you for the Minivers, or against them? For or against? Come on, for or against, or I smash this window." Several other rioters started walking towards them. The hammering on her window redoubled. "Hey, guys! Looks like we've got a fan here!"

"I am not a Minivers fan!" Livia shouted. Her voice was shrill and furious. "How dare you do this? Who do you think you are?" In reply, the boy swung the cricket bat he was carrying against the driver's window. With a deafening crash, the safety glass shattered and flew into the cabin. Livia screamed and flung up her hands to protect her face. The rioter shoved his head into the car.

"Repeat after me. *I hate the Minivers*."

"No."

A hand grabbed Livia's collar. "*I hate the Minivers*."

"I – hate – the – Minivers." Livia could hardly get the words out.

"Louder. Say it again, *I HATE THE MINIVERS*."

"I—" Livia choked. She was so terrified now, she literally could not speak. Livia knew, even if her tormentor had not noticed, that Rosamund and Emily were lying in the back seat under the blanket. If they moved, if they were seen, they would all be torn to pieces. Yet how could she say those dreadful words? Livia opened her mouth, and again they would not come. Instead, the boy leaned suddenly closer and said, in an ominous tone, "Who's that in the back?"

Livia jerked her head around. Emily and Rosamund's faces were still hidden under their blanket, but the covering had slipped and a small foot in a dirty trainer could clearly be seen. Gibraltar, who had said nothing until now, put a firm hand on Livia's shoulder and leaned across to speak.

"It's our children. We've been out all day and they've

been sleeping. Let us pass, please. We need to get them home, you're frightening them." The sound of soft weeping could clearly be heard under the shaking blanket. The boy at the window hesitated. Gibraltar was looking at him, not exactly with contempt, but with the sort of quiet authority that could not be withstood for very long. The rioter looked over his shoulder and saw that several other cars had pulled up in the street behind them. He made an angry, dismissive noise, and jerked his head at Livia to send her on.

"Slowly. Slowly," said Gibraltar, as Livia drove carefully around the bonfire. "Don't let them see that you're afraid."

"I'm not afraid. I'm terrified," said Livia. As she drove past the last of the rioters, even Gibraltar's warning could not hold her back. She flattened her foot on the accelerator and the little yellow car leapt forward and roared away.

Gibraltar leaned over and turned on the car radio. A woman's voice spoke rapidly, reading the news.

"Violent rioting continues across Artemisia tonight, following the discovery that former idols, Rosamund and Emily Miniver, in fact led a secret life of greed and extravagance. The riots began after interviewer Serena Simpson revealed that the Minivers had refused to pay medical expenses for eleven-year-old Alex Burton, the disabled son of their long-standing security chief. Later, a documentary exposed shocking details of the Minivers' private excesses, including a miniature mansion built and paid for by Artemisian taxpayers, an annual catering bill that included fifteen thousand dollars spent on chocolates, and wardrobes filled with designer dresses worth several hundred thousand dollars. Rosamund Miniver, it was revealed, owned more than two hundred pairs of shoes."

"Turn it off!" shouted Rosamund. "Turn it off!"

Gibraltar obeyed. For a moment, there was total silence inside the car. In the last few weeks, Rosamund and Emily had been through every conceivable kind of danger. They had cheated death and won through, against the odds, to be reunited. Now they were facing a threat they had never, in their wildest fears, anticipated.

Rosamund broke the silence.

"So, now we know," she said. "We thought Madame was up to something, and we were right. Madame's stolen our home. She's attacked our friends and destroyed our career, and now she's trying to blacken our names. But she's not going to get away with it. She's not going to take away who we are. This time, the Minivers are going to fight back. As far as I'm concerned, this is war."

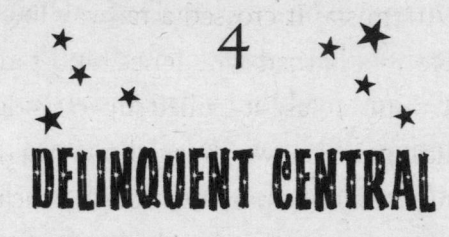

4

DELINQUENT CENTRAL

Fiona Bertram had always been well-behaved. She was sensible and honest, and knew how to say "no" to other people. Fiona had never been in trouble at school, and at home she was the one who stopped her mother, Brenda, doing silly things. Everyone who knew Fiona said she was a good girl. It had never even occurred to her that she might one day find herself in serious trouble.

Now, heading out of town in a police van with a blanket over her head, Fiona could scarcely believe what was happening to her. It was just like the TV news. Only that was different. That was about real criminals who robbed, cheated and killed, not a lonely schoolgirl who was being locked up for helping a friend. Fiona stole a look at Primrose, the guard from Miniver House who was sitting opposite her. She was the hardest looking woman Fiona had ever seen and, despite the blanket, the expression on her face made Fiona feel cold with terror.

The police van drove swiftly until it reached the outskirts of Artemisia. It crossed a railway line, turned through a gate in a barbed-wire fence, and ran along a service road until at last it pulled up outside a long concrete building. Fiona was dragged out and thrust up a flight of steps. As they passed through a heavy door into a corridor, she read a brass name plate at the entrance to the building:

THE QUEEN ROSAMUND
HOME FOR
DELINQUENT GIRLS
ADMISSIONS

Two women, who looked like Primrose's older, meaner sisters, were waiting inside. They took the blanket from Fiona's head and opened a letter Primrose gave them. Cards were stamped and forms filled in. One of the women put a metal tag around Fiona's wrist. It was marked with the letters QRH and a number, like a dog's registration tag.

"Don't take that off," the woman warned Fiona, "or

you'll be disciplined. You'll be in P1. That's where we put the worst offenders," she added, in a voice that made Fiona shiver. "Give her some blues, Margery, and take her through."

To Fiona's relief, Primrose departed. The second woman, Margery, took Fiona to another room where she was made to change into a drab blue shirt and skirt. The clothes were too small and the trainers that went with them were too big, but nobody seemed to care about that. Fiona was given a toothbrush, a nightdress, two sets of grey underclothes, and a change of clothes identical to the ones she was wearing. When she finished changing, Margery threw Fiona's own ragged shorts and top into a bin and took her out into a long passage that smelled of disinfectant.

Margery unlocked and refastened a series of metal gates. *Clang*, went the first gate. *Clang. Clang. Clang.* Each time a gate closed behind her, Fiona felt something inside her shrivel. In this place, she knew she could expect neither sympathy nor mercy. Fiona tried to think of her friend Emily Miniver, who was her age and had gone through far worse than this. It was because of Emily that Titus had sent her here. For Emily's sake, she had to keep quiet.

At the very end of the passage was a door numbered P1. Margery unlocked it, sneering slightly.

"Welcome to your new home," she said. "Good luck. You'll need it."

Four pairs of hostile eyes looked up from inside the room. Margery shoved Fiona forward. The door slammed shut behind her and Fiona Bertram, schoolgirl, of 27 Boronia Drive, Woodside, was a prisoner without hope of escape.

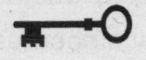

In the darkness on her front verandah, Livia Wallace rocked back and forth in a hammock. Livia always slept outside. During the day she worked in the gloomy basements of the City Archives and she hated feeling shut up in the dark. But tonight, even sleeping outside was not enough. Every time she closed her eyes, Livia smelled the acrid smoke of the bonfire burning in the street and saw the melting faces of Miniver dolls amongst the flames.

Livia was not a Minivers fan. Until recently, she had never given Rosamund and Emily a single thought. Now they seemed to have taken over her life, and she had no way of knowing when, or if, the nightmare was going to end. Livia was not even sure whether she liked the Minivers very much. Emily was at least sweet-tempered, but Rosamund took everything Livia did for granted

Since she had been famous all her life, this was hardly surprising, but Livia still resented it. That Rosamund Miniver, miniature celebrity, might one day soon become Queen of Artemisia, was a prospect she found completely horrifying.

"Queen Rosamund II of Artemisia." Livia tried the title out. She could not really imagine Rosamund ruling Artemisia when Papa King died, but it seemed as if that was what he intended. On her fourteenth birthday, Papa King had given Rosamund his half of the key to the hidden room in the Archives where his will was kept. Everyone, even Gibraltar, agreed that this must mean Papa King intended Rosamund to be his heir. Madame certainly thought so. It was the gift of the key that had sparked off her relentless campaign to destroy the Minivers, and seize the throne for herself. Livia was under no illusions about her cousin. Madame was a mean-spirited, untrustworthy miser and she would make a terrible queen. Yet how could anyone think Rosamund Miniver would be a better choice?

Livia sighed. There was no answer to any of these questions and even thinking about them made her head ache. The front door gave a soft click and Gibraltar emerged from the house, carrying his backpack. Livia sat up in her hammock, alarmed.

"Ssh!" Gibraltar put a finger to his lips. "Emily and

Rosamund have finally gone to bed. They're tired and upset. I don't want to disturb them."

"Of course not," Livia agreed. She hesitated, then asked the question she had been wondering about all night. "Gibraltar. That stuff they said on the radio. About Rosamund's shoes, and that boy. Was any of it true?"

"Some of it was," said Gibraltar. "Unfortunately, that's why it's going to be believed. People don't think: they just believe what they see on the news and read in the papers. A twisted truth is always easier to accept than a straight-out lie and it's going to be very hard to undo the damage. If I'd known, I'd never have brought Emily and Rosamund back to the city. I'm starting to think we should take them out of Artemisia completely."

"When?" Livia tried not to sound too hopeful.

Gibraltar shook his head. "Not straight away. There's something else I've got to do first, and it might take me a couple of days. Tell the girls they must be patient and lie low until I've come back."

"All right," said Livia. "I'll tell them. Good luck, Gibraltar."

"You too."

Gibraltar went lightly down the front steps into the summer darkness. Livia watched him go, then lay back in her hammock feeling bereft and confused. She did not notice the small face at the bedroom window behind her, or realize that Emily Miniver had been listening to every word. She only knew that for all the hardship they had brought her, without the Minivers she would never have met Gibraltar. It was a thought almost too awful to be borne.

Fiona stood with her back to the locked door of P1. In front of her was a dreary room with only one barred window. Two naked electric globes burned on the ceiling, and even they were imprisoned in cages. Four of the toughest girls Fiona had ever seen lounged about on narrow bunks with grey blankets and thin flat pillows, staring up at her, as if she had no right to be there.

Fiona took a step towards the nearest bunk. Its occupant, a scowling girl with a cloud of curly black hair, jumped up and stood threateningly in front of her. A big hulking girl detached herself from a clump at the back of the room and swaggered up to them. Though she was probably not much older than Fiona, she was as tall as a grown-up, and looked like the most brutal sports teacher Fiona had ever known.

"That's Mo's bed," said the large girl. She nodded to the black-haired one, who was glaring as if she was planning something unpleasant. "And that there is Mo.

She's in here because she tried to murder her sister. Of course, Mo says it was an accident, but she's got a very bad temper, so I'm not so sure.

"I'm Bridget. I held up a chicken shop with a replica pistol. And this here –" Bridget pointed to a girl of about twelve with spiky hair and a cheeky expression – "is our famous cat-burglar, Tania. Tania can steal anything. In fact, she probably already has." As she spoke, Tania took a grey object out from behind her back and waved it in Fiona's face. Fiona clutched her pile of clothes and realized that the nightdress was missing from the top. "Up the back, with the ponytail – that's Carla, our resident anarchist. Do you know what an anarchist is, new girl?"

"No." Fiona was scarcely able to speak. Bridget looked at her with satisfaction.

"I didn't either, until Carla came here. Go on, Carla. Tell her what you do."

"I start revolutions," said Carla, in a deep husky voice. "Riots, anyway. I want to end civilization as we know it."

"So, that's us," said Bridget. "What about you, new girl? Why have they sent you to Delinquent Central? It must be pretty bad, if they've put you in P1."

Fiona's face, which was always pale, had gone almost completely white. She made a funny noise in the back of her throat and backed away from Bridget until she hit the metal door. Carla jumped off her bunk and walked towards her with her hands on her hips. Mo made a sort of hissing noise like an animal, and Tania the cat burglar sidled up beside Fiona and wrapped one sinewy arm tightly around her neck.

"Can't hear you," said Bridget.

"The Minivers." Fiona's voice came out in a sort of dry, fluttery whisper. "I'm here because I helped them escape."

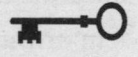

"I helped the Minivers escape."

Fiona repeated the words. As she did, her voice and the conviction that she had done the right thing grew stronger, and she realized with surprise that the four girls were staring at her. Mo stopped hissing. Tania released her hold on Fiona's neck, and Carla, the anarchist, leaned forward intently. Fiona looked at Bridget and saw that her meaty hands were clenched into fists like a boxer's. She clutched her clothes to her chest and squeaked with fear.

Carla gave Bridget a shove. "Bridget! Don't frighten her! Don't you see, she thinks you're going to hit her?" She pushed Bridget aside and stared at Fiona with dark intense eyes. "You know the Minivers? Are they all right? Are they alive?"

Fiona drew in a deep breath. "They were the last time I saw them," she said. "That was two weeks ago. But I think they must still be safe. It was because I wouldn't tell their enemies where they were that they sent me here."

A loud whoop sounded. Somebody clapped, and then the room was full of cheers and shouts of joy. Fiona stared in amazement. Bridget was crying, and Carla, Mo and Tania had flung their arms around each other and were punching the air in triumph. A moment later, Fiona was in the midst of the crush, being kissed and hugged and congratulated. It was unbelievable. For the first time in her whole life, she was a hero.

"Wait!" Fiona cried. "Wait! You have to listen to me!" With difficulty, she pulled herself free from the press of bodies and raised her voice as loud as she dared. "Listen! It's obvious we're all Miniver fans here, but there's more to this than I've told you. The Minivers are in the most terrible danger. I don't know where they are now, but there are people, the same people who put me in here, who want to kill them. They're powerful and cunning, and they're planning something really terrible. I don't know what it is, but it's called Phase Two—"

"Phase Two? You mean all that stuff in this evening's paper?"

"What stuff in the paper?" Suddenly fearful, Fiona pushed forward, and saw Carla pulling back a mattress. She produced a copy of the *Artemisia Telegraph* with a photograph of Ron's son, Alex Burton, on the cover. Fiona took one look at the headline and snatched the paper from her.

"It's not true!" she cried, as she skimmed the story. "It's a lie! It's just not true!"

"Of course it isn't true," said Bridget scornfully. "Do you think we're stupid enough to believe what's written in the newspaper?"

"No way!" said Tania. "You should have seen the rubbish those journalists wrote about me!"

"Even the weather report's a lie in Artemisia," said Bridget. "We only get the papers for the photos of Rosamund and Emily. I've got a hundred and seven pictures of Rosamund in my scrapbook. She's my favourite Miniver, you know," she added proudly.

Fiona was a little reassured. "But how do you get newspapers in here?" she asked. "Surely it's not allowed?"

The four girls exchanged glances.

"We've only just met her," said Tania. "Can we really trust her?"

"Looks like we're going to have to," said Carla. She lifted her eyebrows at Bridget, who cleared her throat and reluctantly nodded.

"All right." Bridget turned to Fiona, looming over her in the same menacing way that had been so frightening a few minutes before. "Swear. Swear that you won't tell anyone inside or outside Delinquent Central what we're about to show you. Swear it – on your own life, and your favourite Miniver's."

Fiona swallowed. "I swear," she whispered. "On my own life, and Emily Miniver's."

Bridget relaxed. "So you're an Emily fan," she said conversationally. "I thought you might be. So is Mo. The rest of us prefer Rosamund, but of course we all really like them both." As she spoke, the other girls carefully and silently pulled one of the bunks out from the wall. There was nothing unusual about the wall behind it, though the skirting board was surprisingly scuffed. Tania knelt and pushed at something. Suddenly, with almost no noise at all, a section of the plaster came loose, and a hole the size of a large dog flap appeared in the wall.

Fiona was amazed. "A tunnel?"

"That's right," said Bridget proudly. "It goes through the wall, past the hospital, then out under the car park to the railway line. We've been digging for nearly six months. We broke through to the surface last Friday."

"Only Tania can get out at the moment," said Carla. "The gap at the end of the tunnel is too small for the rest of us to squeeze through. But it won't be long until we all get through, and when we can, we're going to escape."

"You too, if you're prepared to help," said Tania.

"I've got a better idea," said Fiona. She looked at the others, her fear gone. She had just realized that sometimes, what seem to be the very worst things in life, turn out to have happened for a good reason. Fiona had always been more frightened of Titus than anybody in the world. She knew that he had no heart and no conscience; that he enjoyed tricking people into doing things they did not believe in or want to do, and that when they suffered, he found it fun. That was why he wanted to control Madame, because through her he could deceive the whole of Artemisia. Titus had sent Fiona to Delinquent Central to grind her down and break her spirit, but for once he had miscalculated. Instead of frightening her into doing whatever he wanted, Titus had placed Fiona among friends.

"Emily and Rosamund have been prisoners too," Fiona said. "But they're not like us. They don't have a secret escape tunnel. All they have are the people who love them. Us. We Miniver fans might have been driven underground, but we can help Rosamund and Emily, by putting a stop to *this*." Fiona threw the newspaper on to the floor and gave it a contemptuous kick. "What do you say? Are we going to let the Minivers' enemies get away with this? Or are we going to tell the truth?"

"The truth!" said Bridget, Tania and Carla together. Mo hissed, and the five of them joined hands. The Minivers Underground had officially been born.

5

UNCERTAINTIES

Emily woke under crisp cotton sheets to the smell of lavender and potpourri. Warm sunlight washed into the room under Livia's chintz curtains, and she could see the comforting shapes of the silky-oak dressing table and the moon-shaped mirror on the wall. On the bedside table, a little gold travelling clock ticked on into the morning. Emily lay on her back and stared at the ceiling. Beside her Rosamund slept on, with dried tears on her cheeks. From time to time Rosamund grimaced, as if she were being troubled by an unpleasant dream.

Emily did not want to get up. There was nothing to get up for, only the morning newspapers, and after last night, Emily felt sure these would be better left unread. Part of her still hardly believed what had happened. The riots and the news report had been so horrible, it was as though they were about someone else. And yet, as Gibraltar had pointed out, what had been said was, in essence, true. Even the fifteen thousand dollars worth of chocolates had been bought for a special giveaway. A sick feeling rose up in the pit of Emily's stomach and she rolled over and buried her face in the pillow.

It would all come out. Every bad or embarrassing thing that had ever happened to them, every stupid thing they had ever said. Every bit of mortifying film footage would be dredged up. The sheer awfulness of this, the *unfairness*, was almost more than Emily could stand. How could people go from adoring you to hating you, overnight? Could it really be that love – the love of their fans, which she had taken for granted all her life – was so easily destroyed?

"We're not really like that," said Emily to herself. "Are we?" She thought back to Ron's son Alex. It would have been so easy for them to do something for him. Even the wretched radio-controlled car would have been picked out by one of their PR assistants, probably Penny, the really dopey one, who would never have thought how awful it might look to send a toy car to a boy who had just been hit by one. Emily couldn't even remember signing the card, and the very thought made her want to run away for ever. Yet, even though Gibraltar was thinking of taking them out of Artemisia, the fact that Millamant was still Madame's prisoner made Emily determined to stay. Milly had looked after her and Rosamund when they were tiny babies. She had taught them to walk and talk, had comforted them when they were sad and cared for them when they were sick. Above all, she had loved them, and her love was not the kind that would be swayed by lies or rumours or false reports. In a world gone mad, Millamant was constant and unchanging, and Emily would not, could not, abandon her without a fight.

Emily pushed back the sheets and slid quietly out of bed. She climbed on to a chair and opened the bedroom door, then tiptoed out to the kitchen. Livia was sitting at the table with a pile of folded newspapers pushed to one side. She was writing furiously in a hardcover notebook and seemed not to notice Emily's arrival. Emily moved closer, not liking to interrupt, and suddenly Livia gave a scream and clutched the book to her chest.

"What are you doing? You shouldn't sneak up on people like that!"

"Sorry," said Emily, meekly. "I didn't like to disturb you."

"Well, you did," said Livia, but she was too gentle to hold the grudge, and quickly recovered her temper. "Would you like some breakfast? Don't look at those newspapers: they're quite dreadful. They'll only upset you."

"I'll have to see them some time," said Emily, but her resolve was not yet strong enough to push the point. "I don't want any breakfast, Livvy. I'm wondering if you have a street directory. I want to look something up."

"There's one in the car." Livia looked doubtful. "What are you looking for?"

"Nothing important," said Emily innocently. If it had been Rosamund, Livia might not have fallen for it, but Emily's face did not look as if it hid any sneaky intentions, and Livia did not ask any further questions.

"All right. I'll get it for you," said Livia. She went off to the garage and came back a few minutes later with a dog-eared book.

"Here it is. By the way, Gibraltar's gone away for a day or two. He says you're to lie low until he comes back. I've got to go to work now – can you make yourselves breakfast and lunch?"

"If you can get the cornflakes down for me."

Livia glanced up and saw the box of cereal sitting out of reach on top of the dresser. "Sorry, I keep forgetting. Here you are. I'll see you again this afternoon." She picked up her work dustcoat and stuffed her diary into the woven bag she always carried. A minute later, Emily heard the roar of the yellow car's engine as it reversed up the driveway into the street.

Emily climbed up on to the kitchen chair and pulled the street directory on to her lap. According to Livia, Millamant was being kept in a building called the Bridge

House. It was the old toll-keeper's home at the end of a bridge over the Artemisia River, and it had been empty for many years. Now Madame seemed to have turned it into a sort of secret prison. Emily found the page with the Bridge House on it without too much difficulty but, rather to her disappointment, studying the map did not fill her head with any particular inspiration. She tried to remember what the Bridge House looked like, and pictured a grey stone arch with windows, and a sort of balcony on top. But the details of how many windows there were and whether someone of her size might climb up to them unseen; whether there was a door, and if so, how it was secured, had never even occurred to her. To find out for certain, she would have to go and look.

Emily closed the directory and thought hard. She was not a naturally disobedient girl, and if someone like Papa King or Millamant told her to do something, then she would generally do it. But this did not happen very often. Unlike most girls their age, she and Rosamund were used to making their own decisions, and right now, Emily knew she needed to act. If Milly was going to be rescued it had to be done quickly. The question was, how? Her thoughts were interrupted by a soft footfall and she looked up, and saw Rosamund enter the room. Before Emily had a chance to stop her, she stretched up and grabbed the topmost newspaper from the pile on the kitchen table.

Emily gave a horrified gasp. "Rose! What are you doing? Livia said we shouldn't look at the newspapers!"

"It's too late." As she spoke, the heavy paper came apart in Rosamund's hands. It hit the floor at her feet and left her standing, clutching a single venom-laden sheet. Rosamund stood, staring at the headline, looking exactly like the statue of herself in the TV-6 studio foyer. Emily wondered fleetingly if the statue was even there any more, and then she saw that Rosamund had begun to cry. She jumped down from her chair and prised the sheet of paper from her hands.

It was page three of the *Artemisia Mail*. Half the space was filled with a photograph of Rosamund's shoe wardrobe at Miniver House. A security guard – it was, of course, the treacherous Primrose – stood in front of several racks of dainty shoes with a disgusted expression. Above it, a headline read: *MINIVER OR MONSTER?*

There was no point in avoiding it any longer. For the next few minutes, Emily and Rosamund sat on the floor, trying to make sense of one hateful article after another. Journalists they had known for years, people who had sucked up to them at Miniver House press conferences and fallen over themselves with excitement when they were given exclusive interviews, were suddenly calling the Minivers vile names, and gleefully accusing them of greed and excess. For years, Papa King had controlled the way the newspapers wrote about them. This was payback.

"It says here that neither of us can sing," said Rosamund, pointing to a paragraph on page two. "Miniver Records is releasing a single of me, singing without backing tracks and overdubs, so people can hear how awful I really am. Oh look, Emmie, it's 'Miniver Morning'. It was my very first single. I was only eight years old. Surely people must see how *cruel* that is?"

"Livia's right. We shouldn't be reading this." Emily bundled up the paper and jammed it into the rubbish bin. "There. That's where it belongs. How dare they say you can't sing? You're the most popular singer in the history of the Artemisian charts."

"Oh, what does it matter, anyway?" Rosamund buried her nose between her bare knees, and stared at the lino. "Being a Miniver's such a stupid life. Do you know, Emmie, I used to look at myself in the mirror sometimes and wonder what on earth I was? I used to feel as if I'd come from outer space. Some nights I was so unhappy that I would just lie in my bed and cry until I was almost sick. Only, you were happy, and so was Milly, so I never said anything – only that once, on the night of my birthday party, before all this began. After that, there was never any time to wonder about it. I was too worried about staying free, and finding you again.

"But now –" Rosamund shook her head – "now I don't know what to do any more. I'm not a Miniver, I'm not anything. Everybody hates us and I'm frightened. In a few more years I'm going to be grown up. If I'm not famous, if I'm not a Miniver everybody loves, who will I be? Some weird little *freak* nobody wants?" Rosamund trembled. "What am I going to do? Even if we escape, even if we leave Artemisia for ever, what future is there? Am I going to be like this for ever, two feet high? I don't want to be a Miniver, Emmie. I want to be *normal*."

"Don't say that, Rose," said Emily. "If you weren't a Miniver, you wouldn't be you. And we wouldn't have each other."

"No. Nobody can ever change that." Rosamund hugged her. "Do you know, Emmie, I sometimes think you're the only person in the whole world who really loves me?"

"That's not true," said Emily. She scrubbed the tears from her eyes with the back of her hand. "I don't care what the papers say. There must be some fans who haven't deserted us. People like Fiona, who'll never let us down. And there's Milly. We need to do something about her. In fact – I think we ought to rescue her."

Rosamund looked shocked. "What?"

"I mean it," said Emily. "Rose, please. All this time we've been worrying about ourselves. We've been trying not to think about Milly, because out there in the forest we couldn't do anything to help her. Well, we're back in Artemisia now, and we owe it to Milly to try. At the very least we should go to that bridge place and find out if she's safe. There's nothing dangerous about just having a look."

"I'm not sure I agree with that," said Rosamund. "Anyway, how would we get there? It's much too far to walk."

"Livia's got a car."

"Livia would never take us," said Rosamund. "I'm not sure she even likes me very much. She's always looking at me as if she disapproves of everything I say."

"I think Livia's just worried," said Emily. "Poor thing. It must be horrible, being related to Madame. Livia trusted her, you know."

"I do know she trusted her," said Rosamund, "and believe me, it's not a recommendation." She looked at Emily and considered. "I suppose we could drive the car ourselves. We'd have to think about the pedals, though. Our legs would never reach."

"We'll come up with something. Just think how marvellous it will be to know Milly's safe."

"And how awful if we get caught," said Rosamund, less enthusiastically. "All right. I'll do it, but you must promise me not to do anything dangerous."

A memory of Gibraltar saying they should wait until he returned surfaced briefly at the back of Emily's thoughts, but she pushed it down again.

"I promise," Emily said, and she crossed her fingers tightly behind her back.

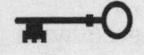

Madame sat up in bed eating her breakfast. It was toast with a scraping of margarine and a cup of weak tea, made with last night's tea bag. Before going to bed, she had carefully tied her fancy new hairstyle up in a scarf in the hope that she would get another day out of it, but the scarf had slipped during the night and several strands of wispy hair protruded from under the edges. Madame wriggled her toes luxuriously under the blanket and, biting into her toast, read every single word of the morning newspapers.

MINIVER RIOTS – MANY INJURED

MINIVER *or* MONSTER?

MINIVER SISTERS' SECRET LIFE EXPOSED

On the front page of the *Artemisia Mail* was a photo of a Miniver doll, skewered on a pitchfork. It was accompanied by a mostly accurate account of the previous night's events. Five people had been injured and one man seriously burned when the petrol he was using to light a bonfire of Minivers memorabilia accidentally set fire to his clothes. Sixty-seven people had been arrested for various offences including damaging buildings and cars, breaking and entering, and brawling. There was also a photo of Madame and Alex Burton. Unfortunately it was on page four, and not nearly as big as she had hoped.

Really, thought Madame disgustedly, was that the best one got for a hundred thousand dollars these days? On the other hand, she could not complain about the amount of space given to exposés of the Minivers' lifestyle. Page after page was filled with articles about their lack of talent, Rosamund's extravagance, and the amazing things found inside Miniver House. Madame found herself particularly disapproving of Rosamund's enormous shoe collection. From the number of pairs she owned, anyone would think the girl was a millipede. A famous author had written a pompous article. *There is nothing remarkable at all about the Minivers: they are simply midgets,* he concluded. *Is this the greatest fraud Papa King has pulled off yet?* Madame frowned a little as she read this, for while she did not respect Papa King, she did not like her father to be criticized when she wanted his position for herself. She put down her toast, and was scribbling a note to remind herself to contact the press office, when she became aware of another presence in the room. Madame gave a little scream. Kitty, her cat, jumped off the bed, and fled.

"You!" said Madame. "How dare you come in here without knocking?"

Titus was standing with his arms folded and his back to the bedroom door. He swaggered over, drew up a chair, and sat down beside the bed. Madame gave him a disapproving look and squirmed away back into her pillows.

"You've got a nerve," she told him. "Who do you think you are?"

"Your PR manager," said Titus. "Chief of Staff, political adviser, and second-in-command. The man who's going to make you queen." He put his hand into his denim jacket and pulled out a small object in a cardboard sleeve. "The new single. Prepared by me in the Minivers' own studio. It's being debuted on Radio Artemisia this morning. I thought you'd like the first copy." He tossed it over. Madame caught it with a crow of delight.

"Is it truly awful?"

"Absolutely dreadful," Titus assured her. "Scarcely a note in tune, in fact. Unimproved, undubbed and unedited, just as it was when Rosamund first sang it. The manager at Radio Artemisia predicts it will be the biggest selling Minivers single ever."

"As long as I get the money," warned Madame. "This is all very expensive, you know."

"You'll get the money, all right," said Titus. "But I'm afraid you're going to have to wait to listen to it. There are a few things we need to talk about, and the first is this." He took out an envelope and passed it to her. Madame shook out a photograph of a brick wall, on which someone had spray-painted the words *MINIVERS UNDERGROUND RULE*.

Madame frowned. "Minivers Underground? What does that mean?"

"We don't know yet. That particular slogan was sprayed on the wall of the Artemisia Cement Works early this morning. Naturally, we've got rid of it, but it's worth noting that the Minivers still have their supporters. We mustn't expect everything to run smoothly."

"It would be much easier," said Madame coldly, "if the people in charge of Operation Miniver had actually managed to find the little brats."

"Another week of Phase Two," said Titus, "and I guarantee that anyone who sees them will instantly turn them in."

"I may not have a week," said Madame. "And there's something else you're forgetting. Rosamund Miniver still has Papa King's half of the key, the key to the Most Secret Room where his will is kept. I need that key, Titus. It's very important."

"I wouldn't worry too much. No one's going to want Rosamund as queen now, no matter how many keys she's been given." Titus suddenly found himself enjoying the conversation hugely. He knew, though Madame did not, that he had snatched the key from Emily at the Artemisia Funfair. At this very moment, it was hanging on a chain around his neck. He decided to fish for more information.

"That relative of yours, Livia. Has she had any luck finding the Most Secret Room?"

"None at all," said Madame. "Livia's not a bad girl, but she's forever drawing and wasting time in the garden when she should be at work. You should see my grand-father's house." Madame shook her head at the horrifying memory. "She's painted it . . . *yellow*."

"Dreadful," said Titus solemnly. "Is that the grand-father who was the City Archivist?"

"That's right," said Madame. "My mother's father, Grandfather Kennedy. He knew where the Most Secret Room was, of course. My mother found out about it from him. Unfortunately, due to some mix-up, she was locked inside it for quite a while, and it . . . affected her. She went very strange. I could never get her to tell me what had happened."

Titus was silent. This was certainly new information. He knew, of course, that long ago Madame and her mother had been banished from Artemisia by Papa King, and that she must have done something particularly treacherous for this to have happened. Titus had always assumed that the records of her crime must be inside the Most Secret Room, and that this was why Madame so badly wanted to find it. But why had Madame's mother, Susan, been trying to get into it all those years ago? It occurred to Titus that it would be very useful to find out more about the reasons behind the banishment. When that happened, he would be able to blackmail Madame into doing whatever he wanted.

Very carefully, for he did not want to arouse Madame's suspicions, Titus said, "That's very interesting. What a shame your mother never told you where the Most Secret Room was. However did she manage to get into it?"

"She stole Papa King's half of the key out of his desk." Madame smirked nastily. "I kept watch for her while she did it. The Archivist's half belonged to my grandfather, but she worked her way around that, too. Look: I'll show you something." Madame opened the drawer of her bedside table and reverently drew out a tiny, ancient tin. She took off the lid, and inside Titus saw some yellow wax, in which someone had long ago left the impression of a key.

"I found it among Mother's things after she died," Madame said. "See the little letter 'A' on the head? It's a wax copy of the Archivist's half of the key. Mother must have pressed grandfather's half into the wax when he wasn't looking. As soon as Livia's found the Most Secret Room, I can have a copy made. But first you must catch the Minivers and get the other half."

"I'm working on it." Titus said goodbye and left Madame to her breakfast. She was, he thought, one of the most stupid people he had ever met. Nevertheless, she was right about one thing. The Miniver sisters needed to be caught. They knew far too much about what he was doing, and they were a problem that he would take great pleasure in eliminating.

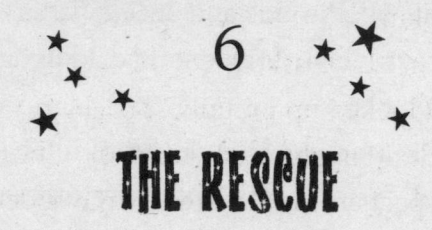

6

THE RESCUE

Livia came home from work that evening feeling tired, grumpy and hot. She'd had an awful day, in which nothing had seemed to go right. Her search for the Most Secret Room was still going nowhere, and she was running out of places to look. Then, halfway through the day, she had received a phone call from Madame telling her to report to the palace at seven o'clock. Livia could not think of an excuse that would not also make Madame suspicious. She had to pretend she was totally on her cousin's side.

It was the sort of evening when she would normally have sat down with a book and some cheese on toast. But when Livia parked the car under the house and clumped up the back steps into the kitchen, she was surprised to smell the scent of cooking. Rosamund was standing on a chair, enthusiastically stirring a great pot that was boiling on the stove. Another saucepan, containing a gloopy tomato mixture, was simmering beside it, and Emily was setting the table with a check cloth and napkins.

"What's that?" Livia asked.

Rosamund looked up proudly. "Spaghetti," she said. "Only I think it might have burned." She stopped stirring the spaghetti and poked her wooden spoon doubtfully into the gloop. Livia dropped her bag on a chair and hastily turned down the stove.

"That's because it's up too high."

"I thought it would cook faster," explained Rosamund. "Never mind. Can you drain the spaghetti for me, Livia? The pot's too heavy for me to lift."

"I'll put your bag in the other room, Livia," said Emily eagerly. By the time she returned from the living room, the spaghetti was in a bowl with the sauce on top, and Livia and Rosamund were sitting at the table.

Livia was genuinely touched. The spaghetti looked disgusting, but it was the first time that Rosamund and Emily had made an effort to help out. Livia took some grated cheese and sprinkled it liberally over the spaghetti to hide the burnt bits.

"I heard something on the car radio coming home," she told the girls as they ate. "Titus has resigned as Vice-President of the Minivers Fan Club. He says he is disgusted by your behaviour and that he's no longer a fan."

Emily pulled a face. "He never was a fan. He told me so himself."

"Pig," said Rosamund. "What's happening to the club? Is anyone replacing him?"

"Yes. A woman called Brenda something."

"Brenda Bertram. She's Fiona's mother," said Emily. "Oh dear. She's so silly, she's sure to be hopeless."

"I wouldn't worry," said Rosamund gloomily. "At the rate we're going we won't have any fans left, so a fan club will be irrelevant."

Livia could not help feeling sorry for her. "Never mind," she said. "Madame's not as much in control as she thinks. She wants to see me tonight, so I'll try and find out what she's up to. Thanks for cooking dinner. I'd better get ready or I'll be late." Livia pushed back her chair and went off to the bedroom to change. She returned about ten minutes later in a clean blue dress, carrying her open handbag.

"Did anyone see where I put my keys?"

"They were in your hand when you came home," said Rosamund helpfully.

"I must have put them down somewhere." Livia started hunting around the kitchen. Emily and Rosamund jumped down from the table to join in the search, but the keys were nowhere to be found. Livia started to become upset.

"I'll be late! Oh, for goodness' sake, where did I put them?"

"Why don't you take a cab?" suggested Emily. "Rosamund and I can look around for the keys while you're gone."

Ten minutes later the keys had still not turned up, and Livia set off for her appointment in a taxi. The Minivers stood waiting on the verandah until the sound of its engine faded up the street. Cicadas chirped in the darkening garden, and in the west, the sunset was marching towards the horizon in vibrant bands of colour. Rosamund crept over and peeped through the lattice. There was no one to be seen.

"All clear," she whispered. "Have you got them?"

"Here." Emily guiltily produced a bunch of keys from her pocket. "I felt so awful stealing them out of her bag."

"I feel awful too," Rosamund admitted. "Do you think we're doing the right thing? When I think of what Gibraltar would say, I just want to curl up and *die*."

Emily hesitated. She knew that Rosamund had great respect for Gibraltar. If Emily had passed on the message about waiting until he returned, then nothing would have induced her sister to leave the house. But staying home would not help rescue Millamant. If Emily or Rosamund had been inside the Bridge House, Milly would have laid down her life to bring them home. The danger was real, but they had to make the attempt.

"We have to go," she said firmly. "We can't let Milly down now."

"No," said Rosamund. "I know that. It's just – I'm so afraid."

Emily tried to sound reassuring. "Don't worry," she said. "It's not as if we're going to do anything. We can't rescue Milly by ourselves. We're only going for a look."

They went inside and dressed in dark clothes and trainers. Emily put two torches into a backpack, and Rosamund carried some cushions and a floppy brimmed hat down to the garage. Luckily Livia had not closed its timber gates, and since the garden was well screened with trees and shrubs, no neighbours could see them. Emily shone her torch over wooden house stumps, the washing machine and laundry tubs, until she found the yellow car.

Something occurred to her. "Does Livia's car have gears?"

"No," said Rosamund. "It's an automatic. Just as well, or we'd never be able to drive it." She opened the driver's door and plumped the cushions down on the seat. While she operated the handbrake, Emily pushed the seat forward as far as possible. Emily climbed on to the seat, then on to the stack of cushions. Rosamund made a face and slid into the well under her feet.

"I don't know why it has to be me who operates the pedals," she complained.

"Because you're an awful driver," said Emily. "Remember – right foot, press the accelerator. Left foot, press the brake."

"We're going to crash, you know," said Rosamund fatalistically. Emily pulled the floppy hat down over her too-famous face and started the engine. She put the car into reverse and carefully let off the brake, using both hands and all of her strength.

"Accelerate," she ordered, and pressed her right foot down on Rosamund's shoulder.

The car shot violently backwards. There was a deafening bang and a jarring impact. Emily shrieked and Rosamund yelled as she hit her head on the steering wheel. They had not just crashed the car: they had crashed it without even leaving Livia's garage.

"Oh, no!" Emily opened the door. She had driven straight into a wooden house stump. The car had a huge dent in the right rear panel, and the stump was splintered and knocked askew. They were lucky the damage wasn't worse, but there was now no way they could keep what they were doing secret.

"That's done it," said Rosamund, rubbing her head. "When Livia gets back, we're really in for it. Oh well, nothing ventured, nothing gained, as Milly always says." She sat back down in front of the pedals and Emily closed the door. With difficulty, the two of them drove the car forward away from the stump, then reversed, very carefully, up the driveway and into the street. Emily found the headlights and switched them on. She put the car into Drive, and headed off in the direction of the river.

The trip to the Bridge House was slow and nerve-wracking. Emily had picked a roundabout route that went mostly through backstreets, but they could not avoid busier roads completely, and their jerky progress made her horribly afraid of being noticed. Luckily, the car had power steering, which made the enormous steering wheel easier to manage, and the traffic was quieter than usual, perhaps because people had been scared by last night's riots. Nobody seemed to notice them, and eventually they approached the bridge from the southern side.

"Rose. We're nearly there."

Rosamund grunted. It was not much fun operating the pedals, and she was starting to get cramps in her legs from sitting jammed up at Emily's feet. Emily drove over the bridge in a stream of traffic. She went under the arch that contained the Bridge House and turned left into a street that ran along the riverbank. Emily pulled on to the verge and killed the engine. She slid over on to the passenger seat and helped Rosamund out from under the steering wheel.

"Get out this side, Rose: it's safer." Emily opened the door, and hopped cautiously out. The grass along the riverbank was neck high, and since the street lamps were on the other side of the road, it was relatively dark. Emily and Rosamund locked the car and crawled through the grass towards the bridge. About fifty metres away from it they stopped, and sat for a moment looking up at their goal.

At either end of the bridge, an arched building spanned the roadway. The one at the southern end housed the machinery which opened the bridge to let large boats through. The northern arch had been where the toll-keeper lived, who had once collected travellers' money. No one had lived in the Bridge House for a very long time and it was a sinister looking place. Nevertheless the building still had windows, and a blue door at the foot of one of the piers.

"They must have taken Milly in through that door," said Rosamund in a low voice. "Look: it's out of sight, underneath the road. No one would even have noticed them arrive."

"Let's go closer." Emily inched her way forward through the grass until they reached the foot of the pier.

The door was lit by an orange lamp on the underside of the bridge and there was a gravel driveway that led down from the main road above. Emily could see at once that to leave the shelter of the grass for the driveway would be far too dangerous. Even if they reached the door without being seen, it would almost certainly be locked. Emily felt a rush of frustration.

Rosamund touched her arm gently. "Come on. Let's go around the back and see if there's something there."

She wriggled off through the grass and Emily followed. The ground sloped steeply down to the water, becoming soft, then squelchy, and the grass got thicker and lusher. Emily and Rosamund stood cautiously upright. At the back of the pier was a blank wall. It had neither windows nor doors, but a couple of rusted gratings were set into the stonework.

"It's no good, Emmie," whispered Rosamund. "Come on. We shouldn't hang around. It's not safe."

"Wait a moment." Emily pulled her torch out of her backpack and turned it on, shading the glow carefully with her hand. She handed it to Rosamund, who pointed it at the wall. The dim light flickered over the gratings.

"There's a way in. Look!" Emily said.

Rosamund paled. "You're not serious!"

"Please, Rose. It's a chance, a way in—"

"And it's not going to go away. Emily, you *promised*

me. You said we were just coming for a look—"

"But Milly's inside there!" An image of Milly, alone, suffering and imprisoned, suddenly flooded Emily's head. All sense of her own safety vanished, and she began tugging at the grating. The rusted metal broke and crumbled in the centre. Emily thrust a stick into the hole and started working it back and forth like a lever. Rosamund grabbed her wrist, and they tussled for a moment in the grass.

"Listen to me! There'll be someone inside there! If you get caught, what'll I do? I'll never get away on my own, Emily – *stop!*" Rosamund's hushed voice rose to a squeak. Emily did not listen. She redoubled her efforts with the stick, and the rusted grating suddenly broke and gave way.

"Rose, please. Let me look. I won't do anything silly. This may be our only chance. You keep watch out here, I'll be as quick as I can."

"And what if I do see something? How am I going to let you know?" Rosamund demanded. Emily's head and shoulders were already disappearing into the hole. A moment later her feet vanished after them. There was a faint scrabbling sound, then nothing.

Rosamund sat helplessly on her haunches, looking at the gap where her sister had gone. She felt terrified, and more angry with Emily than she had ever been in her life. If it hadn't been for Emily, she would never have even left Livia's house. Rosamund was furious with herself for not stopping her. Who did Emily think she was? *She* was the oldest sister, the one Papa King had chosen to be queen. Rosamund half-stuck her head through the grating, but it was so dark inside she immediately pulled it out again. Hating herself for being a coward, she gave up, and crept back up the riverbank to keep watch over the gravel driveway and the door.

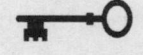

Emily emerged on the other side of the grating into a cold, dank space. At first she did not have any idea where she was. Her courage, which had propelled her through the gap, almost deserted her.

Emily knew she had made Rosamund very upset. She also knew that she was doing something Gibraltar had specifically told her not to do. Milly herself would not approve. Emily could almost hear her voice in her head, saying sternly that she was not to put herself in danger. But Emily had made her choice and there was no going back now. With trembling hands, she shone her torch over the rough, rather damp concrete under her feet and took a hesitant step forward.

The torch was not a very bright one, and it was hard

at first to work out where she was. Then her light settled on a metal ladder. Emily began to climb. It was not very pleasant climbing a ladder that had been made for someone with normal-sized legs, especially in the dark, but the ladder was not a long one, and she soon reached a trapdoor. It opened on to a small cellar, from which a flight of concrete steps led up to a room at street level. This room was empty, apart from some wooden boxes, and the rumble of traffic going over the bridge was so heavy that Emily could scarcely imagine how anyone had ever lived here.

The stairs continued up to the tower rooms above. Laboriously, Emily began to climb again, all the way to the top floor. On the final landing was a closed door. Emily's heart started pounding. The knob was too high for her to reach, but she tried anyway, straining her fingers until they just touched it. The knob rattled slightly, and she redoubled her efforts. Then a voice, so small it was like the rasping of a dry leaf on a pavement, sounded anxiously on the other side.

"Who's there?"

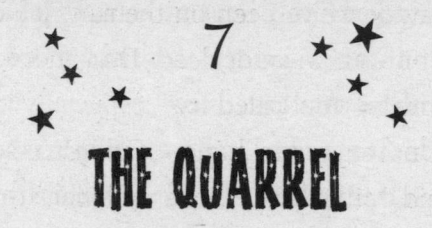

7

THE QUARREL

"Milly?" Emily's voice came out in a low waver. "Is that you?"

There was silence for several seconds. "Emily?" The raspy voice spoke again from the other side of the door. "What are you doing here? You shouldn't have come, you *shouldn't*." The sentence broke off in a fit of coughing. Emily tried to peer under the door. It was dark on the other side, but she had her torch and she shone it recklessly through the crack. The dim light did not help much, but when she slid her slender fingers into the gap, another hand, a familiar hand with short stumpy fingers, grasped hers as if clutching a lifeline.

"Milly? It's me, Emily. Are you all right?"

"I am now you've come," said Millamant. "Emily, I've been so worried about you! To hear your voice – it's a miracle. Quickly, tell me, what about Rose? Is she safe, too?"

"Rose is fine," said Emily. "She's keeping watch

outside. We came here looking for you. Ever since they took you away, we've been on the run. We didn't know whether you were alive or dead. Do you know Madame tried to pretend you killed us?"

"No. On the other hand, it doesn't surprise me, either," said Millamant. "She's evil, that one. She was always trouble, from the time she was a girl." Her fingers tightened on Emily's. "Be careful, little Emmie. From the moment Madame came back to Artemisia I was afraid for you, but there was nothing I could do. Has she made herself queen yet?"

"Not yet," said Emily. "But she's trying very hard, and she's doing her best to get rid of us. Especially Rosamund. We think it's because of that key Papa King gave Rose for her birthday."

"The key is very important," said Milly. "It opens a secret room in the City Archives that has all sorts of things hidden away in it. Tell Rose that she must keep the key safe at all costs. If it comes to the worst, you might be able to bargain with it."

"I'm afraid it's gone," said Emily in a very small voice. "I've lost it. It was stolen."

Milly patted her hand. "Never mind. It's a pity, but it's not the end of the world. Do you know, Emmie, I'm very proud of you and Rosamund? I was terrified that you'd both get caught, but it seems to me that you've been leading those people of Madame's quite a dance."

Emily smiled briefly. Millamant continued, "And now, dearheart, I want you to leave. There's nothing more you can do for me, and it's too dangerous to stay. You and Rosamund must leave Artemisia. As long as Madame is in control here, you are in great danger. She plans to kill you; I know, because she's told me so herself. You mustn't be tempted to try and rescue me, or stay in the city because of me. Promise me that, whatever happens, you and Rose will put your own safety first."

"You can't expect me to leave you!" Emily exclaimed. "Milly, I came here to save you!"

"My darling, that's beautiful, but I'm afraid I'm way past saving," said Millamant calmly. "I've been ill ever since I got here; I couldn't even walk down the stairs. No, Emily. I'm glad that you're free – I can't tell you how much that means to me. But it must finish here and now. Say goodbye, quickly, and then you must go."

"I *won't*." Emily squeezed Millamant's hand so tightly that her own fingers burned with the pressure. "I won't leave you. I can't give up, not after all that's happened—"

"*Ssh!*" said Millamant. A door opened below, one or two floors down. "There's someone coming!"

Rosamund was scared, bored and angry. It was a particularly nasty mix of feelings. By insisting on going inside, Emily had put them both in danger. While she was in the Bridge House, Rosamund could not leave her post for an instant, yet if somebody turned up unexpectedly, what on earth was she to do?

It was all Emily's fault. Rosamund did not understand what had happened to her sister, but she was very aware that, in the weeks since they had gone on the run, Emily had changed. In the past, because she was the elder sister and the most popular Miniver, Rosamund had always known she was in charge. Now Emily had somehow grown up, and Rosamund felt as if she was being left behind. The girl who had been content to be the second Miniver, who had happily followed in Rosamund's wake, was gone, it seemed for good. The new Emily was still sweet and thoughtful, but there was a steely determination in her that had not been there before. Rosamund was secretly dismayed by how willing this Emily was to make her own decisions and suggestions about what they should do. Even worse, her decisions were often the right ones. What did it matter now that Rosamund was good at choosing songs to sing or clothes to wear for their next TV appearance? None of that counted for anything any more, and Rosamund, sensing her control slipping away from her, felt Emily slipping too, and was resentful, angry and afraid.

The sound of an approaching car engine interrupted Rosamund's thoughts. There was so much traffic noise overhead that it took her a moment to realize that a vehicle was driving down the gravel service road from the road above. Rosamund dropped flat among the clumps of grass. A dark van swung off the driveway under the bridge and pulled up outside the blue door at the foot of the pier. The engine died, the headlamps switched off, and two men got out. Rosamund clapped her hand to her mouth to stifle a gasp. One of the men was Ron Burton, whose sandy hair and weather-beaten face she had last seen on television. The other was Titus, the former Vice-President of the Minivers Fan Club.

Ron reached into the van and took out two or three folded blankets. Titus had a rope over his shoulder, a thin rolled-up cord that for some reason frightened Rosamund more than any weapon. As she watched, Ron took a key from his pocket and unlocked the door at the foot of the pier. It opened inwards and the two men went inside.

Rosamund's head bobbed up among the clumps of

grass. She was so panic-stricken that when she tried to stand up, her foot caught in her long T-shirt and she almost fell over. Rosamund picked herself up and ran to the door. It was shut, and the handle was far too high for her to reach. She gave it a useless shove, and immediately realized that she was being extremely stupid. If Emily was trapped inside the Bridge House, the last thing Rosamund wanted to do was attract attention to herself. If she was going to help her sister, she would have to think, and think fast.

Rosamund put her hand into her pocket. There was a penknife in there that Gibraltar had given her when she and Emily were hiding in the cave. Rosamund flipped out the biggest blade and ran down the steps to Ron and Titus's van. For someone as small as she was, Rosamund was unusually strong. Part of this was due to the enormous amount of dancing she had done since she was very young, but part of it was simply the way that Minivers were made. Rosamund was much tougher and fitter than an ordinary child of her height and weight, so it was no trouble at all for her to plunge her knife into the van's tyres. The air hissed out of the cuts in a satisfying way, and the van began to tilt and settle as the tyres flattened. Whatever else they did, at least Ron and Titus would not be able to follow her and Emily when they drove away. It was a poor sort of insurance, but it was better than nothing.

Rosamund crept back to the door. She was wondering again how she could get inside when a hand came down unexpectedly on her shoulder.

"I don't think going in there would be very wise," said Gibraltar.

"What's that noise?" said Emily. Her hand was still holding Millamant's under the door and she felt Millamant's fingers begin to shake. Emily could tell she was very frightened.

"It's the downstairs door. Someone's come; Emily, you *must* go. Find Rosamund and get away, or they'll catch you!"

"No." Emily was not going to leave now. It was because she had left Millamant behind in Miniver House on the night they had gone on the run that Milly had been taken prisoner in the first place. Hoping that Rosamund had been able to keep out of sight, Emily let go of Millamant's hand and slid into a crack between some wooden packing crates full of papers that were stacked against the wall. There was a small space there, just big enough for a Miniver to turn around and crouch in. It was terribly dusty and dirty, and a splinter grazed her leg, but with luck nobody would think to go looking.

Emily sat listening. Two people were talking in low voices as they came up the stairs. When they reached the top, there was a rattle of keys and Milly's door creaked open.

"What have you been up to?" said a man's voice. "We left you on the other side of the room." Emily could not quite hear Millamant's reply, but when a second voice spoke, she felt a chill drop straight to her stomach and stay there.

"You were talking to someone," said Titus. "We heard your voice."

"I was talking to myself!" Millamant's voice raised anxiously. "I've been here on my own all this time. I've got nothing else to do."

"Then you must be going mad from being locked up." Titus sounded as if the prospect pleased him. He had not entered Milly's cell, but had been talking to her from the doorway. Now he stepped back out on to the landing and Emily almost stopped breathing. From within her hiding place she could see Titus's trainers and the leg of his shabby jeans. His feet took a few steps towards the crates where she was hiding and she pressed back, willing herself to disappear into thin air, oblivious to the splinter that was sticking into her side.

Then she heard the flick and rustle of paper, and realized that Titus was not looking for her. Instead he had been distracted by the contents of the crates, and was looking through some of the papers.

"She can't walk, Titus," called Ron from inside the room. "Shall I carry her down to the car?"

"Better tie her up first." To Emily's enormous relief, Titus shoved the papers back in the crate and went into Millamant's prison. There was some low conversation which Emily could not hear, but from the groans that followed she guessed that Milly was being tied up, and that Titus and Ron were doing a thorough job of it.

"All right, that'll do," said Titus. "We ought to dope her, too, just to be on the safe side. The kit's in the car, isn't it?" The two men moved away, and Emily heard them going downstairs again. It would only be moments before they returned, but it was a chance Emily had to seize. Without a moment's hesitation, she wriggled out of her hiding place and ran through the open door into the tower room where Milly was being held.

It was horrible beyond anything she had imagined. There was no bed, no running water, not even the ghost of a breath of air. Milly was lying in the middle of the room where Ron and Titus had left her, like a little caterpillar in a roll of blankets. Emily gave a cry of distress and started clawing at the swathes of cloth.

"Milly!"

"Emily, what are you doing here?" White and haggard, Milly's face emerged from the folds of blanket. "I told you to leave, and I meant it. It's too late to do anything for me now. Even if I wasn't tied up, I'm too weak to walk."

Emily burst into tears. "How could they do this to you? I hate them, I hate them, I *hate* them."

"None of that," said Millamant sternly. "Turn the other cheek: that's what I've always taught you. Now, you must go, Emmie. Kiss me, quickly, and give my love to Rose."

Emily flung her arms around Millamant's neck.

"You always were a good girl," Millamant said. "I'm proud of you. And this isn't goodbye, you know. I will try and get away, and when I do, I will come and find you. Where should I look for you?"

"With friends." Emily struggled to remember Livia's address. "Seventeen Daventry Street, Artemisia West."

"Seventeen Daventry Street," Millamant repeated. "I'll remember. Bless you, Emmie, and goodbye."

Emily nodded. She knew she could not linger, so she blinked back her tears, gave Millamant a kiss and slipped back out on to the landing.

Emily ran lightly down the stairs. There was no sign of Ron or Titus, but she kept a watchful eye out, fearful that they might return. At the bottom of the stairs was the trapdoor she had entered by. Emily had intended to go out the same way, but she saw now that the front door was open, too, and the sound of shouting told her that something outside was going very wrong.

The voice was Titus's. Emily ran to the open door, and to her astonishment, she saw Gibraltar and Rosamund. Gibraltar was fighting off Ron and Titus, doing his best to keep them away from Rosamund with a branch ripped from a tree, but he was outnumbered, and Ron was a trained security guard who knew how to fight. He was dodging every swing of Gibraltar's branch and making careful feints that were getting closer to him with each step. Aghast, Emily stared at them, and then suddenly Rose darted over, grabbed her viciously by the arm and dragged Emily down the painted concrete steps.

"Come *on*!" Rosamund hissed.

"But what about Gibraltar?"

"We have to leave him. He told me to find you and run. I know how to do what I'm told, even if you don't!"

Her fingers gripped Emily's wrist so tightly there was no resisting. Together, the Minivers darted around the pier into the long grass, running so fast for the car that Emily almost stumbled over her own feet. She managed to pant, "But what's Gibraltar doing here?" and then they reached the car and Rosamund was wrenching open the door and shoving her inside.

Rosamund answered, as she jammed the keys into the ignition. "He came to rescue Milly, of course. Only *you* wrecked everything. Milly's still a prisoner and probably Gibraltar is too by now, and it's all *your* fault. Sit still and shut up. I'm driving this time, and if you dare say anything else to me I think I'll *hit* you!" She shoved Emily on to the floor, jumped on to the seat and slammed the door. Rosamund's hard little foot came down on Emily's right shoulder. Almost blinded with tears, Emily pushed down on the accelerator pedal, and the car shot forward crazily on to the street.

Rosamund had always been a terrible driver. In their Miniver House days, she had crashed her special Miniver-sized car more times than either she or Emily cared to remember, and back then she had not been terrified and furious. Livia's car sped dangerously down the backstreets by the river, veering around bends, its engine rattling like a rocket about to take off. Emily could only pray that they would not crash. Then Rosamund's left foot came down on her shoulder and she jammed on the brake, bracing for the impact as her sister swerved to the side of the road. Sure enough, there was a jarring bump, and the car came to a standstill. But Rosamund had merely driven off the road into a grassy ditch. A moment later she had pulled on the handbrake and grabbed Emily roughly by the shoulder.

"Get up. I want to speak to you."

Emily clambered out of the footwell, dishevelled and slightly breathless. Rosamund gave her a shove and she landed on the passenger seat.

"What do you think you were doing back there? You promised me – you *promised* me – that we were only going to look."

"But Milly was in there—"

"We knew that before we even left Livia's. That was why we went there. To have a look, you said. You went in, when I had no way of following you or getting you out if something went wrong. You could have got both of us killed or caught. I told you not to do it, and you went ahead and did it anyway."

"Since when have you told me what to do?" demanded Emily hotly. "I don't have to do what you want. Just because you're older than me doesn't make you the boss, you know."

"*I'm* the one Papa King gave the key to. I'm the one who's going to be queen—"

"Well, you're not queen yet!" Emily yanked her arm out of Rosamund's grip. "Let me go! You reckon you're so grown up and clever. What makes you think you can rule Artemisia when you can't even drive a car?"

"I can drive!"

"You can't. You can't do anything for yourself. From the moment you left Miniver House, you've had people to look after you. I had no one. I had to hide from Ron and his team, and Titus and Madame, all by myself. And I did it, because I wasn't afraid to take risks. That might have been our one and only chance to rescue Milly—"

"It *was* our only chance, and you blew it!" yelled Rosamund. "I told you, that was why Gibraltar was there, you idiot! He was trying to get Milly out, and if you hadn't been there, he would have. Now Milly's been taken away, and Gibraltar's probably a prisoner, and it's all your fault." She burst into a storm of weeping. "If they've caught Gibraltar, I shall never forgive you, ever!"

The violence of her outburst shocked Emily into silence. In all their lives, Rosamund had never spoken to her like this before. It was as if some stranger was unexpectedly inside her sister's skin, struggling to get out. Emily watched the tears rolling down Rosamund's cheeks and felt suddenly frightened. If Rosamund, too, was abandoning her, then what was left? An unseen future, in which the Minivers were no longer sisters, but two small and lonely people who no longer thought and acted as one?

Her voice came out as a whisper. "I'm sorry, Rose. I was wrong. I'm sorry."

"You're not sorry." Rosamund was still crying. "And I don't want your apology. Not unless you mean it. I always knew you were cleverer than me, but I never thought you'd treat me as if I was *stupid*."

"That's not fair, Rose, I do mean it," began Emily, but before she had a chance to finish what she was saying, a bicycle pulled up beside the driver's window. The door opened and Rosamund, who was leaning against it, almost fell out on to the ground.

"Need a driver, ladies?" asked Gibraltar.

8

THE MINIVERS UNDERGROUND

"This isn't good enough, Livia. This just isn't good enough," said Madame. "You've been searching for the Most Secret Room for months. Do you really mean to tell me you still haven't got a clue where it is?"

"I'm afraid I don't know, Cousin Karen," said Livia. "I know it's taking a long time, but the Archives building is very big. I'm sorry. I just haven't been able to find it."

The two cousins sat on either side of Madame's desk. Livia hunched her shoulders and lowered her eyes meekly. Somehow it was always easy to underestimate Madame when she was not in front of you. There was something ludicrous about her constant preening and primping, and her desperate desire to be famous. It was a different matter when Madame was actually there. Then you realized that underneath the faintly ridiculous surface was a cruel and ruthless woman who would stop at very little. Livia was sure Madame knew she was deceiving her. It was clear she was starting to run out of patience.

"Stop pretending, Livia," said Madame. "You're not sorry at all. Personally, I think you're not even trying. If you had been, by now you would have produced some results."

"Perhaps the Most Secret Room isn't even there," suggested Livia. "We don't know for certain, after all. Perhaps it never even existed."

"It exists, all right," said Madame coldly. "Our grandfather had the key. He knew where it was, and so did my mother."

"She didn't tell you where it was, though," said Livia, with a flash of the spirit that Madame found so annoying. "If it's so important, I wonder why you didn't ask her."

"By the time I needed to know, she was too ill to explain," said Madame. The fact that her mother had been as mad as a hatter after the experience was a family secret she had no intention of sharing. "I didn't want to distress her. It's up to you now, Livia. The time for messing about has passed. You're going to have to search in that bottom basement."

Livia blanched. "The ninth basement?"

"You heard me," said Madame. "You should have started there in the first place. It's the obvious place to look."

"But it's horrible down there." For the first time, real anxiety filled Livia's voice. "It's dark. There's no electric light. Nobody ever goes down there; nobody. They don't even keep any records in it. It's empty."

"Then it won't take you long to make a thorough search," said Madame. "No more excuses, Livia. You've held me up for far too long already."

Livia bit her lip. She knew that Madame was probably right. An empty basement that nobody visited was the obvious place for the Most Secret Room to be hidden. Nevertheless, Livia knew that she could not go down there. The ninth basement was the deepest and most horrible of the Archive's underground levels. She had heard stories about staff who had strayed down there, got lost, and never returned, or who came back, days later, as gibbering idiots. Livia was scared of the dark, and so afraid of being shut up that at work she had regular panic attacks. She dared not say so to Madame, but she could not, would not, obey her. She would think of some excuse, and if necessary she would lie.

"Very well, Cousin Karen," Livia said at last. "I'll do my best."

"Your best so far has been pretty hopeless," said Madame. "Come back next Tuesday with a full report. If you don't, I'm warning you, there'll be consequences."

Livia drove home to Daventry Street in a taxi. *I wish I knew how to get out of this,* she thought, as the cab sped westwards. *I can't fob Cousin Karen off for ever. She's already suspicious, and if she finds out I'm helping the Minivers, she'll probably kill me. If she was prepared to murder her own father, Papa King, why would she think twice about me?* Livia closed her eyes in near despair, but there was no easy answer. In two days' time she was going to have to go back to Madame and pretend she had searched for the Most Secret Room in the bottom basement. That meant more lies, more secrecy and more fear.

The taxi pulled up at her address and Livia paid the driver and got out. The lights inside the house had been switched off, which rather surprised her, for it seemed far too early for Emily and Rosamund to have gone to bed. Livia went up the front path and climbed the steps. Without her keys, she could not get in, so she rapped smartly on the door and waited for an answer. There was none. Something was clearly very wrong.

In rising panic, Livia ran down the steps to the driveway. She knew she had left the garage open, and that there was a spare house key hidden beneath the laundry tubs. Livia fumbled for the light switch. The fluoro blinked into life and she reeled back against the wall, horrified.

Her car was gone. One of the house stumps had

been almost smashed in half, and there was an ominous scrape of yellow paint along its broken edge. Livia stood for a moment, so shocked she could scarcely take it in. Then she took a step forward, and her foot nudged against a small object lying on the ground beneath the broken stump. Livia picked it up. It was a small tin, very old, that had once held sweets of the sort her Grandfather Kennedy had been fond of, and that he had often given her when she was a little girl. There was something else inside it now, a metal object that rattled when she gave the tin a shake. Livia started to take off the lid, but at that moment a car with a familiar-sounding engine turned into the driveway, and she mechanically put the tin away in her pocket.

The car rolled down the drive. It came to a stop inside the garage and the driver pulled on the brake and turned off the engine.

"Gibraltar!" Livia ran to the driver's door. Gibraltar flashed her a reassuring smile. He turned to the back, where Emily and Rosamund were sitting, uncharacteristically silent, on either end of the seat. Livia stared at them.

"What have you two been doing?"

"Ask Emily," said Rosamund savagely. "It was *her* fault, not mine."

Livia's eyes fell on the smashed-up panel at the back of the car and she let out an involuntary scream.

"My car! You little wretches. *What have you done?*"

A few streets from the Royal Palace was the biggest railway shunting yard in Artemisia. It was a place where empty freight carriages were stored, and trains were coupled together and held until needed. At two o'clock in the morning, all was quiet here. The last passenger trains had left for the night, and though there were still a few freight trains passing through on the up line, there was nobody about on the tracks.

A big, slow coal train came rumbling through the darkness. It was so long that it needed several minutes to clear the shunting yard, and as it clicked over the rails past the darkened sets of waiting passenger carriages, a flicker of movement showed in one of the cars. Dark shapes slid and clambered over the rim of the coal-filled hopper, dangling briefly before jumping to the ground. There was a soft crunch as trainered feet hit the clinker, and the intruders quickly separated. One ran off into the shadows on the hill above the shunting yard, a second headed for a small wooden hut. Two more moved rapidly among the trains waiting on the sidings. There was a metallic shaking sound followed by a soft hiss, and, as if by magic, words began appearing on the carriages' silver flanks.

Fiona coughed as she accidentally inhaled the fumes from her spray can. "Ugh. This stuff *stinks*."

"It does, doesn't it?" Bridget spoke in a hoarse whisper, her right arm sweeping up and down in a practised arc. "You get used to it, though. Just don't breathe too much in, or you'll throw up."

Fiona giggled. "Imagine if they saw us doing this, back at Delinquent Central."

"If you don't watch out, they will," said Bridget. She pointed warningly to a closed-circuit security camera that was angled on a pole overhead. "Those things are everywhere. Be careful."

"Sorry." It occurred to Fiona that being a competent delinquent needed quite a bit of practice. She shook her spray can and started squirting a wobbly message across the silver metal of the next carriage. Bridget was already working on her third slogan. *Stop the Lies! Give us Back the Minivers – Free the Minivers – We Love the Minivers*. At the end of each message, Bridget sprayed the letters *MU*, for Minivers Underground. In a few hours' time, when the rush hour started, the trains would be carrying their messages all over Artemisia.

"*Make Yours a Miniver Morning.*" Bridget came up and

read Fiona's slogan approvingly. "I love that song."

Fiona nodded. "Me too. It was Rosamund's very first hit."

"*Cute.*" Bridget tossed her empty spray can over her shoulder and took a new one out of her backpack. Her fingers were covered in red paint. Fiona saw that her own were now streaked blue. She hoped no one back at Delinquent Central would notice.

"Bridget, Fiona — look at this!" Tania came around the corner of the carriage, lugging a plastic box. "It looks like some sort of explosive. I found it over there in that shed."

"Do you think it's safe?" asked Fiona anxiously.

"No idea," said Tania. "But you never know, it might come in useful."

Bridget rolled her eyes. Given the chance, Tania would bring back anything she could lay her hands on. Every time she said that it "might come in useful", but the others all knew that really, Tania just liked stealing things.

"Well, if you must take it, don't let Carla see it," said Bridget. "You know what she's like with things that go bang. She might decide to start a revolution and I don't trust her not to blow herself up. How's she going?"

"Nearly ready, I think," said Tania. "Look — there she goes now."

The three of them turned and looked up on to the

hillside above the yard. A smell of petrol and flames wafted towards them and they saw Carla's small dark figure running down the slope. Behind her, gigantic fiery letters were springing into life, burning brightly in the night, and leaving scorch marks in the grass for everyone in Artemisia to read:

Minivers Forever

"Ha! Let's see what Madame thinks about that," said Bridget with satisfaction.

When the members of the Minivers Underground had set off on their late-night mission to the shunting yard, the fifth delinquent, Mo, had been left behind at Delinquent Central. There were a number of reasons for this. Officially, Mo had been told to guard the tunnel entrance and keep watch over the exit, which could not be opened from the outside. Unofficially however, Mo had been left out because the others did not quite trust her to behave herself on such a delicate mission. Mo did not think: she just reacted, and sometimes she even surprised herself with the crazy things she did.

Mo was not very happy about being left behind. Even

by the standards of Delinquent Central she was a slightly scary person, but it was not very nice to find that the others preferred to take Fiona, who had only been there two days. Mo felt hurt and lonely. Why couldn't she do something for the Minivers, too? She was sure she loved Emily and Rosamund just as much as the others did. As she wandered up and down the tunnel, dark resentful thoughts started creeping through Mo's head. Suppose she shut the others out, and used the tunnel to escape herself? That would serve them right for leaving her behind. The idea grew with frightening rapidity, and Mo had almost made up her mind to do it when the sound of human voices floated unexpectedly down from the building above.

Mo froze in her tracks. As far as she could make out, she was somewhere under the hospital. Because the girls at Delinquent Central were all young and healthy, it was usually empty, and she could not understand why there was anybody there so late at night. Yet there were definitely people moving around, and a yellow light clearly showed through a wire grille in the wall. Mo climbed up on to a piece of broken concrete and tried to peer into the room above. Her view was restricted, but she could just distinguish three people. One was the Delinquent Central Governor, popularly known to the girls as Sharkface, and the second was the hospital

Matron, Squelchy. The third person was a young man, a stranger. He had fair rumpled hair and was wearing black jeans and a T-shirt.

"Do you want to see the prisoner?" said the young man. He gave a rolled-up bundle on the floor a little kick. It groaned softly, and Mo realized that it was a person, swaddled tightly in blankets like a corpse.

"No, thank you." Sharkface's voice was stiff. "I have to say, Mr Titus, this is extremely irregular. This Home is under the authority of the Artemisia Prisons Board. If they get word of this—"

"They won't," Titus assured her. "And if they do, I assure you that my authority will override theirs. No need to stand on formality, by the way. Plain 'Titus' will do, and may I call you . . . Hattie?"

If the danger had not been so real, the thought of the Governor being called Hattie would have made Mo burst out laughing. Squelchy knelt and started unwrapping the bundle of blankets. The prisoner groaned again and gave a terrible rattling cough.

"She's pretty sick, I'm afraid," said Titus. "Just try and keep her alive, if you can. It would be inconvenient if she died just now."

Squelchy felt the prisoner's pulse. "She's in very poor shape," she said disapprovingly. "I'd say she's got pneumonia. I'll have to put her in the ward. There aren't any other patients, so it should be safe."

A trolley was found, and the prisoner lifted on to it. Mo saw that the person under the blankets was very small indeed, about the size of a toddler, and obviously not heavy. What sort of prisoner was this, a miniature inmate so secret that she could not go through the normal admission procedures? Suddenly Mo was struck by a terrifying realization. There were two people in Artemisia who were that important and that tiny, and they were Rosamund and Emily Miniver.

The two women wheeled the trolley away. Left behind to wait, Titus sat down on a chair and stretched out his legs. He was looking at nothing in particular and after a while he began humming softly under his breath. At first, Mo could not quite work out what the tune was, but then he began tapping out the rhythm on a side-table near his chair, and she realized that it was "Miniver Morning".

Mo was hard to scare. She had seen and done a lot of bad things in her life, and had been in more trouble than she could remember, but something about the way Titus sat and tapped and hummed was more than just creepy: it was sinister. Mo realized that Titus must be the enemy Fiona had spoken of, the person who was trying to destroy the Minivers, and who had sent Fiona to Delinquent Central. She had said he enjoyed deceiving people, in making them do wrong things, in making them suffer. Mo knew she had to do something to stop him, but she could not think what. As Mo watched, Titus's face changed. It took on the shape of Rosamund's features until he almost *was* Rosamund, mimicking her at her most temperamental and ill-behaved. Then Rosamund was gone, replaced by an Emily who was not quite Emily, and Emily was followed by someone else Mo did not know, but whose face was vain and mean and stupid altogether. So quickly did the impersonations follow each other that it was hard to tell when one stopped and the next one started. Mo was transfixed. She stood, clinging to the grille like an animal whose gaze was held by a snake, and then suddenly something happened. Her foot, which was balanced precariously on the bit of concrete, wobbled slightly and pitched her forward.

The movement made the slightest of noises, but Titus heard. His expression went instantly blank, and he stood up, looking around the room for the source of the sound. Mo felt faint with terror. She stared at Titus, waiting for him to see her behind the grille, and as she looked at his face she realized that she had never before seen so complete a void. It was as if she was looking inside the real Titus and there was nothing there: no emotion, no compassion, and no conscience. Instead, into the vacuum that lay at his heart, all kinds of evil had been drawn and made their home.

Titus's eyes fell on the grille. He took a step towards it, and then the door opened behind him, and Sharkface and Squelchy came back in. Titus swung round to them enquiringly, his face once more dressed up in its pleasant smile.

"I've put her on a drip," said Squelchy. "She should be comfortable for the rest of the night. We'll tell the other staff she has to stay in isolation because she's infectious."

"Good," said Titus. "Thank you, ladies. We'll let matters rest there, and I'll be in touch with you tomorrow morning."

The three of them turned off the lights and departed. As soon as they had gone, Mo went to find a jemmy. A deft wrench pulled the hospital grille from its place, and she scaled up the wall and through the opening. Was the prisoner Rosamund, or Emily? Hoping desperately it was Emily, she gently pushed open the swing door into the ward.

A weak voice called out from inside the room. "Who's that?"

Mo stopped with her hand on the door. The excitement that she had been feeling turned to bitter disappointment. She had never met either Rosamund or

Emily Miniver, but she knew their voices as well as she did her own. Whoever was in the bed was not a Miniver. It was not even a girl's voice, but a woman's.

The prisoner called out again. "Who is it?" This time, Mo entered the room and went up to the bed where the voice was coming from. A small and extremely plain woman was lying in it, hooked up to a drip and looking very ill. She had blonde hair, blue eyes, and a snub nose, and at the sight of her, Mo's heart began to pound. The prisoner was neither Emily nor Rosamund, but Mo had seen her picture many times in *Minivers Monthly* and knew she was the next closest thing.

She was Millamant.

9
COUNCILS OF WAR

Emily had not thought it possible that things could get worse after their disastrous visit to the Bridge House. She soon found out that she was wrong. All of a sudden, it seemed that everyone was angry with her. Gibraltar was annoyed that she had been irresponsible and ignored his instructions, and Livia was furious about her car, which she could not afford to have repaired. As for Rosamund, she was angry with Emily about everything, and nothing Emily could say or do seemed to make the slightest bit of difference.

By bedtime, Rosamund was still not talking to her. Worse followed. As soon as Emily entered their bedroom, Rosamund pointedly picked up her pillow and went to sleep on the living room sofa. When Emily tried to talk her round, Rosamund screamed and threw a hairbrush at her. This brought down a lecture from Livia and sent Emily running for the bedroom to cry over the injustice of it. Nothing in her past life with

Rosamund had equipped her to cope with such behaviour. It was simply inexplicable.

The next morning was Saturday. At breakfast, Rosamund would not eat with Emily, would not speak to her, and would not look her in the eye. Instead she curled up in the living room with a book – Rosamund, who was famous for never reading anything but the fashion hints in *Artemisian Vogue*. Emily locked herself in the bathroom and sobbed herself into near hysteria. After that, she kept to herself and tried not to talk to Rosamund at all.

For as long as she could remember, Emily had looked up to her older sister. She had loved her, admired her, and secretly wanted to be like her. Emily had always known that Rosamund was the most popular Miniver, yet she had never resented this for an instant, because in a sense she was Rosamund's biggest fan herself. It had been Rosamund who had patiently helped Emily with her dancing, Rosamund who encouraged her when she was making her first recording, Rosamund who told her what clothes and make-up to wear, and how to cut her hair. From the moment their nightmare adventures had started, all that had mattered to Emily was that she and Rosamund should be together. Of course, Emily had known that she was doing the wrong thing in deceiving Rose, but she had hoped the fact that she was doing it for Millamant would make a difference. She now knew she had been wrong. It was not that Rosamund did not care about Milly's fate: quite clearly, she did, or she would not have gone to the Bridge House in the first place. What she could not forgive, it seemed, was the fact that Emily had ignored her position as the elder sister. Rosamund was accustomed to being the leader and Emily had tricked, ignored and disobeyed her.

The stand-off lasted until Saturday evening. By then, Emily had spent the whole day more or less by herself. Gibraltar had gone to get clothes from his caravan, and Livia had spent her day in the garden in a frenzy of pruning and mulching. She had come back inside at six to cook an uninteresting dinner of fish fingers and frozen chips, and when they had eaten it, she left the table without a word and started running a bath. Emily sat at the kitchen table, looking mutely at the tablecloth. When she glanced up, she saw that Rosamund was looking straight at her.

Rosamund finally broke the silence.

"I want you to know," she said, "that I'm not angry with you any more. I was angry last night. What you did wasn't fair. It could have been the end for both of us. I don't care about that, though. I don't even care that you hurt my feelings. What I care about is the fact that we stopped being a team. You just did what you wanted without even worrying about what I thought. You behaved as if I didn't count for anything. I might as well not have been there."

"I'm sorry." Tears seeped out from Emily's eyelids and ran down her cheeks, but the relief of finally talking to Rosamund was so great that she did not care about the lecture. "It was just that I wanted to find Milly. She was so close, and I couldn't bear it. It never occurred to me that Gibraltar would try and rescue her. Honestly, I never dreamed it would happen."

"Neither did I," said Rosamund. "But I would have done what Gibraltar wanted and stayed back here, if you'd only passed on the message. That's another thing. I don't think you realise how important Gibraltar is in all of this. You'd hardly even met him when we left for the forest, but I spent a whole week hiding with him. I know he can seem mysterious, but I've been through enough to be sure that he understands exactly what he's doing. You've got to listen to Gibraltar's advice, Emily. If you try and do things your own way, we'll all end up worse off than we can imagine."

"I do listen to Gibraltar, and you, too," said Emily.

"It's not that I'm trying to make you do what I want, Rose. I've just got used to making my own decisions."

"Well, you can't do that any more," said Rosamund. "We can't make decisions without telling each other; there's too much at stake. Besides, if anyone's in charge it's me, not you. I'm the eldest, remember. I'm the one Papa King gave the key to; I'm the one he wants to be queen when he dies. I know I'm not ready for it, not yet, and maybe never, but Papa King is the only father I've had, and if that's what he wants, I'm not going to let him down. But I can't do that if my own sister lies to me. Do you understand, Emily? I have to be able to trust you."

"You can trust me," said Emily. "A hundred per cent, Rose. I promise."

"A hundred per cent, then," said Rosamund. "I believe you. But that's not enough, Emmie. There's something else you have to agree to. If I'm going to be a queen, it's time I started acting like one. From now on, I'm completely in charge of what we do. I'll always ask for your opinion, but I must have the final say. Promise me, or this simply isn't going to work."

Emily sat, stunned. Rosamund's expression was perfectly serious; it was clear she had meant every word she'd said. Emily did not know how to reply. She trusted Rose – of course she did. She would lay down her life to save her without a second thought. But this was not about trust, or sacrifice. It was about Rosamund pulling rank as the elder sister, when being the eldest no longer mattered. Everything screamed out to Emily that promising to obey Rosamund in a real crisis could be a disaster. Yet the memory of their argument still hung between them like smoke after a fire, and Emily knew she could not risk this happening again. For the sake of her love for Rose, for the sake of their future as Minivers, there could be only one reply.

"All right, Rose," said Emily reluctantly. "I promise. From now on, you're in charge."

Rosamund exhaled. Until that moment, Emily had not realized she had been holding her breath, or known how desperately anxious her sister had been. She reached out her hand and felt Rosamund grab her fingers like a lifeline.

"Oh, Emily," she said, and her voice dropped to a whisper, "it's been so awful not being able to talk to you. I have to show you something. I found it in Livia's handbag when I was putting back her car keys, and I just don't know what to think." Rosamund put her hand into her pocket and handed Emily a small rusty tin. The lid was printed with the words *LION MINTS*, and an old-fashioned picture of a peppermint plant.

"What is it?" Emily opened the tin and stared at the contents. "What – Rose, how on earth could Livia get this?"

"That's what I thought, too," said Rosamund in a frightened voice. "It is my key, isn't it? The one Papa King gave me for my birthday? I don't understand how Livia found it. I thought Titus stole it from you."

"He did." Emily fingered her throat, where Titus had ripped Rosamund's key from the string on which she had worn it. There had been a bruise on the back of her neck for days afterwards. "Livia was at the palace last night. Do you think she might have got it from Madame?"

"If she did, then why hasn't she said something?" demanded Rosamund. "Emily – do you think Livia can be trusted? She's so strange and difficult sometimes, and I'm sure she doesn't like me. Could she be on Madame's side?"

"I don't think so. If she was, she would have handed us over long ago." Emily turned the key over in her fingers and examined it. She had worn Rosamund's key around her neck for the best part of a week, and this certainly looked like the same one. On the other hand, the key to the Most Secret Room had been deliberately made in two pieces, and only worked when the halves were joined together. Papa

King's half had been given to Rosamund. Was it possible that this was the other?

Emily put the key into the tin. "We have to put it back," she said firmly, and then, remembering her promise, added, "That is – if you think it would be a good idea, Rose."

Rosamund was slightly flustered. "Yes – yes, you're right, we should. Livia's bag's over there, beside the dresser." She jumped down off her chair and she slipped the tin back into the front pocket of the bag. As she did, a soft footstep sounded outside on the back staircase, and was followed by a gentle rap on the kitchen door.

Emily and Rosamund froze, like rabbits caught in the headlights of a car. The back door was closed, but not locked, and its top half was filled with a lattice panel, through which any normal-sized person could easily peer. The tap sounded again, and a girl's voice spoke through the lattice.

"Emily? Emily, are you there?"

The fear dropped from Emily's face like a shutter. She ran to the door and started jumping up and down, trying to reach the knob. Rosamund ran instinctively to help. The door flew open and two girls in drab blue clothes burst excitedly into the kitchen.

"Emily!" cried the smaller of them. She dropped to

her knees and Emily flung her arms joyfully around her neck.

"Fiona! Fiona, it's you!"

The kettle was on the hob and the introductions had been made. Gibraltar had come home, and now they were all sitting at the kitchen table, eating cake and biscuits. Livia filled her biggest teapot with tea leaves and poured on the boiling water. She carried it over to the table and set it down on a trivet to brew.

"Have another piece of fruit cake," she said to Fiona and Bridget.

"Yum," said Bridget. She had already eaten three pieces. "Do you think we could take some home to Delinquent Central?"

"If there's any left," said Livia. "The way we're going, I think you'll be lucky."

"To think I'm eating supper with the Minivers," said Bridget happily. "Cool."

She looked across at Rosamund with an awestruck expression. Rosamund smiled back. The discovery that she still had fans was like healing balm poured into her soul. Admittedly, it was disconcerting that their main fan base was now operating out of a girls' home, but meeting Bridget and hearing about the Minivers Underground had cheered her and Emily up immensely. The fact that Fiona was working with her made them even happier. Fiona had helped Rosamund and Emily escape from Operation Miniver, and was a true friend. Besides, she had brought with her a piece of news that made everything else seem unimportant. Millamant was alive and safe in the Delinquent House hospital. She was the person who had told Fiona and Bridget where to find them.

"So you see, it wasn't a waste, your going to the Bridge House," said Fiona triumphantly. "If you hadn't spoken to Millamant, we would never have learned where you were." Rosamund said nothing, but Emily could not resist a glance in her direction that said "I told you so".

"Tell us more about the Minivers Underground," Emily said aloud. "Have you managed to get in touch with any other fans?"

"Not yet," said Fiona regretfully. "It's really difficult, working out of Delinquent Central. There are only five of us and we can't leave the home during the daytime. We've done all we can, but we can only manage so much."

"It's still a brilliant idea," said Rosamund. "You've done much better than we have." Fiona and Bridget both looked pleased.

"That's true enough," said Gibraltar, speaking for the first time. "But I think, now Fiona and her friends are involved, that it would be a good idea to talk about what happens next. It's not sensible or practical to have two groups working separately. If we're to achieve anything useful, we need an overall strategy."

"You mean, we should pool our resources?" asked Livia.

"Yes," said Gibraltar. "But before we do that, we need to agree on what we are trying to achieve. Are we fighting for the Minivers' survival? Or are we fighting to defeat Titus and Madame? The two things are linked, but not quite the same. Before we can go on, the time has come for Rosamund and Emily to start making some decisions."

Emily and Rosamund exchanged glances. "Decisions?" Rosamund asked. "What sort of decisions?"

"Decisions about your own future," said Gibraltar. He took the teapot in his strong hands and twisted it. "It's a bit like making tea, you see. Leave the pot too long and the leaves stew. Pour too soon, and the tea's too weak to drink. It's a matter of timing, of knowing exactly when to pour."

"You're saying," said Rosamund, "that the time has come for Emily and me to pour?"

"Not exactly," said Gibraltar. "But I am saying that

you're moving towards that more quickly than you realize. If you and Emily don't make choices now, someone else will make them for you. How long do you think you can stay here in this house? A week? Three days? A few hours, even? We just don't know. But sooner or later, someone will notice something. Livia knows that. Every time a car drives by, she jumps; when she hears a bird or a possum in the garden, you can see in her eyes she thinks it's Madame. And she's right to be afraid. Madame's spies are everywhere; she has almost the whole population of Artemisia on her side. Everyone is looking for the Minivers, and sooner or later, no matter how careful you are, somebody will find you. One slip-up: that's all it will take. That's why you need to decide what you're going to do. Do you want to run for ever? Or do you want to reclaim your lives, and start fighting back?"

"Fight back, of course," said Rosamund. "The only problem is, how? We're so small, and there's only two of us."

"Seven," put in Fiona firmly. "The Minivers Underground is right behind you. Besides, it's only your bodies that are small. As far as your fans are concerned, you and Emily are the biggest people in Artemisia."

"The most famous people, yes. That's not exactly the same thing."

Emily suddenly sat forward.

"No, Rose," she said. "Fiona's right. The other night you called this a war, but it's a war for people's hearts and minds, for the way they think. Where that's concerned, you and I are as big and strong, and have as much experience, as anybody. The Minivers Underground is on the right track. We have to find a way of joining with them and hitting back against Madame's lies. We need to put the record straight."

"But how?" demanded Rosamund. "You know, it's all very well for you to say that, Emmie, but we're not as clever as you seem to think. When we were famous, we had a whole press office to deal with that sort of stuff. We just gave interviews, or turned up at the TV station, and the whole thing was managed for us. You're talking about getting in touch with the whole population of Artemisia. To do that properly means a broadcast on TV or radio, and there's no way that's going to happen. It's simply impossible."

"Why?" said Bridget. "Nothing's impossible if you really want to do it. Look at the Minivers Underground. We dug a tunnel out of a high-security building. Why shouldn't you do a broadcast?"

"We'll help you," put in Fiona.

"That's very kind," said Rosamund. "But I still don't see how we could do it."

"A TV broadcast would certainly be very difficult," said Gibraltar thoughtfully. "Television stations have extremely tight security; the moment you entered the building, you'd be caught. On the other hand, with careful planning I think we might pull off something on the radio. It will be dangerous, though, and it will get harder the longer we leave matters. Madame intends to rule Artemisia, and her position is growing stronger every day. She is trying to make people love her, the way they have always loved the Minivers. The question is, are you prepared to let her do it? Are you prepared to see Madame become queen?"

"No!" said Rosamund at once. "No, I'm not. Papa King gave that key to me. I'm not going to roll over, just because Madame's fighting dirty. We're not cowards, you know."

"I never thought you were," said Gibraltar. "There is a choice, though. If you don't want to fight, you can always leave Artemisia. It won't be the first time someone's gone into exile."

"That would be running away," said Rosamund. She shook her head. "I'd much rather try the broadcast. Someone needs to tell the truth. Besides, it's not just about us any more. Look at poor Fiona, locked up just for helping us. Madame has Milly in her power, and Papa King, too. The moment we were out of the way, I'm sure she'd kill them both."

"You're right, there," said Gibraltar. "The fact that Papa King is old and sick wouldn't stop her for an instant. It would just make it easier for her to murder him." He turned to Emily. "What about you, Emily? Rosamund said she wanted to fight back, but is this what you want, too?"

"Of course it is," said Emily. She looked at Rosamund meaningfully. "Rose and I are in this together. I'm behind her, one hundred per cent."

10

SECRET PLANS

At nine o'clock on Monday morning, an orange taxi pulled up outside the Artemisia City Archives and a single passenger got out. It was Titus. With his canvas backpack and shabby clothes, he looked like a student. In a sense, this was exactly what he was. Titus had taken time off from running Operation Miniver to do some research behind Madame's back.

Titus walked through the big bronze doors into the Archives foyer. Most people found their first visit to the Archives unnerving, for there were no windows and inside the building was dark and claustrophobic. Titus, however, was rarely troubled by atmosphere. Like Livia and Madame, he was hunting for the Most Secret Room, but because he was going about it in a different way, he was much closer to finding it than they were.

From the very start of his search, Titus had known he did not have much time. Unlike Livia, who was a member of the Archives staff, he did not have access to the basements where the records were kept, and he was also anxious that his investigations should not attract Madame's attention. Madame was suspicious about everything nowadays, and Titus knew that Ron did not trust him either. The longer he spent in the Archives building, the more likely it was they would find out. Besides, Livia had already been searching the place for months. Titus assumed that if there had been something in the basements, by now she would have found it. The hiding place had to be somewhere else, in some part of the building where Livia had not yet searched, or to which she did not have access. To find out where it was, he simply had to ask the proper person.

Titus walked up to the reception desk. "Good morning," he said to the girl on duty. "My name is Titus, from Operation Miniver. I'm wondering if I could have a word with the City Archivist."

"I'm afraid you can't see Ms Milton without an appointment."

"I won't take up much of her time," said Titus. He gave the receptionist his most charming smile. "It's very important that I see her. Look: here's a letter from Madame, authorizing my visit." He handed over an envelope and the girl opened it. It contained a letter he had written himself on stationery stolen from Madame's office, but, as Titus had expected, the receptionist was completely taken in. Her manner changed at once and she hopped off her stool.

"Please wait, sir." She disappeared, and came back a minute or two later with a serious young man.

"Mr Titus? I am Tom McMahon, sir, Ms Milton's assistant. We can give you ten minutes. Please come this way."

Tom McMahon led Titus up a flight of stairs to an imposing door marked CITY ARCHIVIST. Titus waited while he was announced, then walked into a huge white office. A dark-haired woman was sitting behind an enormous desk covered with perspex business trophies. Ms Glenda Milton had been City Archivist for three years. She had succeeded to the position on the death of Livia's Grandfather Kennedy, and a large plaque on the wall announced that she had just been given an award for Bureaucrat of the Year.

"Good morning, Mr Titus," said Glenda Milton. She picked up his letter and waved it at him. "I'm told this is important. I hope it is. I am a very busy person."

"It is important," said Titus, "and since I'm a busy person too, I'll come straight to the point. Papa King is very ill and likely to die. His will is stored in the Archives. I have been sent by Madame with instructions to go to the Most Secret Room and look at it. Here is

Papa King's half of the key which opens the door. I believe, as City Archivist, that you have the other."

Titus put the half key on the table. Glenda Milton stared at it.

"I beg your pardon," she said. "What Secret Room is this?"

"It is the room where Papa King keeps his confidential papers," said Titus. "Papa King and the City Archivist are the only people who know where it is."

Glenda Milton burst into tinkling laughter. "Oh, no!" she said. "No secrets here. In this modern age, we must have Accountability. Accountability, Availability and Access is our motto."

"Access is precisely what I'm asking for," said Titus. "I want to know the location of the Most Secret Room. Can you tell me where it is or not?"

"I've never heard of it," said Glenda Milton. "My predecessor never mentioned it, and he certainly never gave me a key. Between you and me, the old fellow was quite gaga. Things have changed a lot since his time. Manage, Modernize and Move On, that's my method. What's been done in the past is no concern of mine."

"Really? I would have thought the past was very much your concern," said Titus sarcastically. Glenda Milton looked blank. Titus decided to give it one last try. "Has Papa King ever been to the Archives himself?"

"He has no need to," said Glenda Milton proudly. "Trust, Transparency and Truth are our organization's watchwords. Papa King has the utmost confidence in my management."

"I'm sure he does," said Titus, mentally adding Glenda Milton's name to the list of people he would have sacked as soon as possible. He left her and found his own way down to the public reading room.

It was a setback, but Titus was not deterred. To find the right person was clearly going to require a bit more effort, but he was good at ferreting out information. He already had a backup plan prepared. Titus wrote a list of the files he wanted on a stack slip and handed it to the archivist on duty. About fifteen minutes later, a porter came by with a trolley and handed him several ancient folders tied up with pink tape.

Titus took the folders to a study booth and worked steadily for about an hour, making notes in a firm clear hand on some sheets of paper. Around lunch time, he sent back the files and asked for more. By two o'clock, he had covered three pages with a list of names taken from the records of the Artemisia Works Department. They were builders, carpenters, plasterers and electricians, and they all had one thing in common. Seventy years before, in the days of old Queen Rosamund, they had helped construct the building in which Titus now sat.

One sheet of names was headed *APPRENTICES*. These people had been very young when they worked on the project, and Titus knew it was more than likely that some were still alive. It was simply a matter of looking them up in the phone book. Titus tucked the list away in his backpack, put the files he had been using on a trolley, and left the building. In the Archives forecourt, Glenda Milton was being photographed with some VIPs.

"Relevance, Research and Renewal," she was saying. "Under my management, the Artemisia City Archives are moving forward into a New Era." There was a polite scatter of applause and Glenda Milton smiled at the camera. She did not notice Titus: in fact, she had forgotten all about him. Somebody else had not, however. As Titus walked off towards the palace, Tom McMahon watched him go with suspicious eyes.

Down on basement level four, Livia's telephone gave a sharp ring. Livia put down her pencil and stared at the handset, willing it to stop. Her workmate, Gavin, looked up from the opposite desk in annoyance.

"For goodness' sake, Livia. That's the third time that phone's rung in the last twenty minutes."

"I'm busy."

"So am I. Just answer it, will you?"

Livia sighed and picked up the receiver. "Livia Wallace."

"I'm wondering how you're going with the ninth basement," said a voice on the other end. It did not bother to say hello. "I've been waiting all day. I haven't heard anything."

"I haven't had a chance to look yet," said Livia. She had never expected Madame to wait until Tuesday for news about her search, and was not surprised it was her. "I can't talk now. I'm doing something important." She hung up. The phone immediately started ringing again. Livia leaned over to pull the plug out of the wall and the frayed wire snapped with a shower of sparks. Gavin jumped.

"That'll teach her." Livia shoved back her wobbly chair and took a torch out of her drawer. "I'm going down to the lower levels," she announced to Gavin. "I've got to look for something. I might be a while."

"You're always snooping around down there," Gavin grumbled, but Livia had heard his complaints before, and did not hang around to listen. She headed off to the main staircase, looking braver than she felt. What had Madame thought when she heard the telephone go suddenly dead? Part of Livia could still hardly credit that she had hung up on her, but even though she knew that Madame would not let the insult pass, she was glad that she had done it. On Friday night, something inside Livia had changed. When she had discovered her grandfather Kennedy's key in the garage at Daventry Street, she had realized that for the first time in her life she was no longer powerless.

The tin containing the key was in her pocket now. Livia was not quite sure why she had kept her discovery secret. She had, at first, been so angry about what the Minivers had done that she had not wanted to talk to anybody. Later, there had been no reason to keep silent, yet Livia had continued to hug the news to herself. Why had her grandfather hidden the tin in the garage rafters at all? It was as if he had deliberately left the key for Livia to find, at the time in her life when she most needed what it could give. A good locksmith could surely make a full key based on the half she had. And if she could find the Most Secret Room without Madame knowing, Livia could use the information it contained to do anything she wanted. She could stop Madame becoming queen. She could force her to have Millamant and Fiona released from Delinquent Central. She could even buy safe passage for Millamant, Emily and Rosamund out of Artemisia. Then, when Papa King died, the Parliament of Artemisia would pick a suitable successor – Livia was not sure who, but it would certainly not be Rosamund – and there would be nothing left to worry about. Madame would be finished, the Minivers would be gone, and she and Gibraltar. . .

All this time, Livia had been making her way down through the lower basements. Each level was darker and more stifling than the one before, and her torch made less and less light the further she went. The smell was awful. Livia put her hand into her pocket and felt the tin to give herself courage. At last she reached the eighth level. It was a horrible place, and there were not even any records there to speak of, for no one had the courage to carry them down there. Sweating and fearful, Livia followed the chalk marks she had made on the walls on her previous visits, until the corridor she was walking down reached a dead end, and stopped. Painted in flaking paint on the concrete wall was a shaky number nine, and an arrow pointing towards a hole in the floor.

She was standing at the top of a narrow metal staircase. There were no proper lights in this part of the building, but the darkness coming up from the level below was so deep and dreadful that Livia's torch barely lit the first step. Livia began to tremble. She felt a wave of nausea rise up in her throat, but she could not tear herself away from the top of her staircase. Everything

137

she feared most was down there, the darkness and the closeness, the horror of oblivion, and the terror of death. Livia put her foot on the first step. It disappeared as if it had been cut off at the ankle, as if she had stepped into a pool of living ink.

Livia closed her eyes. She remembered the Most Secret Room and all the reasons she needed to find it. She thought of her little house with its sunshine-coloured walls, of her garden with its flowers and vegetables, of her embroideries and drawings. She thought of the ideas and hopes she had recorded in her diary, and she thought of Gibraltar. She pictured his face and tried to hold on to her dreams. But they were fading fast, and even for Gibraltar, Livia knew she could not do it. The ninth basement had defeated her. Her torch dropped from her fingers and fell into the hole, and she turned and fled towards the light.

"What's the matter with you?" said Gavin, as Livia came running into the workroom. "You look like you've seen a ghost."

"I'm fine."

"You don't look fine," said Gavin doubtfully, but Livia ignored him. Something had to be done, and it could not wait. She sat down breathlessly at her desk, found her fountain pen, and began to write:

Dear Cousin Karen –

Livia lifted her pen. She read what she had written, screwed up the first sheet of paper, and began again:

Dear Madame,
Following your instructions on Friday evening, I have now visited the ninth basement to look for the Most Secret Room. Nothing I have seen makes me think that it will be found there.
As you know, I have been searching the Archives very thoroughly for several months. I have now looked in all the places I am allowed access to, and have no choice but to give up the search. I am very sorry that I have not been able to find what you wanted. I have done my best, and hope you are not too disappointed with me.

Yours sincerely,
Livia Wallace

Livia read her letter through one last time. It sounded very stiff and formal for something written to a relative, but nothing on earth would have induced her to tell Madame this news in person. In any case, she did not care if she never saw her cousin again. Livia put the letter into an envelope, addressed it, and put it into the mail tray for the palace. Tomorrow morning was Tuesday. By the time Madame received it, the Minivers would be almost ready to strike.

"We've got the field radios you wanted!" said Bridget jubilantly. She and Fiona came into Livia's kitchen, staggering under the weight of two heavy plastic crates labelled *AAF* for Artemisia Armed Forces. "Short-wave radios, and a transmitter. Carla and Tania liberated them last night from an army supply dump!"

"Yes, I heard about that on the news," said Gibraltar dryly. "They said something about an explosion, so I knew it must be you."

"Tania got the dynamite from the railway shunting yard," explained Fiona. "They didn't use much. Nobody was hurt."

She took her place beside Bridget at the kitchen table. Emily and Rosamund were already sitting there with Livia and Gibraltar. There was excitement in the air, and a slight feeling of tension. Since the meeting on Saturday evening, plans for Rosamund's radio broadcast had quickly taken shape. They had chosen a radio station, Radio Artemisia, and picked a time for Tuesday night. The girls from Delinquent Central had assembled all the equipment that was needed. Tonight was their last chance to plan their attack and make sure all the details were correct.

"Let's get on with it, shall we?" said Gibraltar. "I am very aware that this is only our second meeting, but I also know that if we don't move now, we may be too late. The longer Phase Two is allowed to go on, the harder it will be to reverse the damage. Tomorrow night, we hit back hard. If anybody disagrees with this, now is the time to speak out."

He looked around. Everyone was silent. Gibraltar nodded, and went on.

"Good. Right from the start then, it has seemed to me that this idea of a radio broadcast has one big flaw. As soon as any illegal transmission begins, security teams will surround the radio station from which it is being made and attempt to stop it. We know the people we are up against are completely ruthless. It will certainly be dangerous for any of us found inside the station building, and for Rosamund or Emily it would probably be fatal. For this reason, it seems obvious that Rosamund has to make her speech from another location and patch it through for broadcast. It's simply not practical to do it from Radio Artemisia itself."

"I want to do it from Miniver House," explained Rosamund. "Emily and I have our own studio there, in one of the turrets. We used to do radio interviews from there all the time."

"You want to make your broadcast from Miniver House?" asked Fiona. "Why? Won't they just catch you there instead?"

"If everything goes according to plan, they won't know I'm there," said Rosamund. "I will be at Miniver House, speaking on the telephone, but the *broadcast* will be transmitted from Radio Artemisia. Hopefully, Operation Miniver will assume I'm there."

"It sounds awfully risky to me," said Livia doubtfully. "Are you sure you can operate the equipment?"

"It would be easier if we had our sound engineer," admitted Rosamund. "But I know the set-up, and I'm sure I can make it work. The dangerous part will be breaking into the building."

"Why not put your speech on to a tape instead?" suggested Emily. "That way you wouldn't even have to go there."

"I thought of that," said Rosamund. "You're right, it would be safer that way. But if I'm going to do this, I have to be willing to risk something. I want our fans to know it's really me. I want the phone lines open, so that they can ring up and ask me whatever they want. I want the chance to explain myself. To do that, it has to be a live broadcast. This is our one chance, Emmie. We may never get another. We have to get it right."

"Rosamund and I have made some preliminary plans," said Gibraltar. "Everybody will be assigned a specific task. Fiona, Bridget: you and your friends will need to arrive at Radio Artemisia around ten o'clock tomorrow night. That's when the night shift starts, so you should be able to break in quite easily. Barricade yourselves into the studio and get ready to follow our instructions. I'm sorry, but it's quite likely that some of you may be caught. Will that be a problem?"

Bridget shrugged. "The worst they can do is send us back to Delinquent Central," she said. "We're used to that. Besides, we can always organize another escape."

"Just don't fight back if you can help it," warned Rosamund. "I don't want anyone getting hurt because of me. Livia: we're going to need you to drive the getaway car to and from Miniver House. You'll need to wait in the street and be ready to leave as quickly as possible. That leaves one last job. This plan is only going to work if the timing is absolutely precise. For that reason, we need somebody to direct the attack. Our operations coordinator will need to make sure everyone is in position, and give orders over the field radio for the various units to move. I suggest the best person to do this will be Emily."

"Me?" Emily exclaimed. "But I don't want to! I want to go with you to Miniver House."

"Well, you can't," said Rosamund flatly. "We need somebody to do this job, and you're the obvious person."

"Why?" demanded Emily. "Because I'm the youngest? Or because you're still angry with me? You made me promise to do what you said, Rose, and now you're trying to get back at me for what happened at the Bridge House. It's not fair. I won't do it, do you hear me? *I won't.*" She jumped down from the table and dashed out of the room.

"Wait! Emily, wait!" Rosamund scrambled down off her chair and ran after her. The sound of violent weeping could be heard coming from the front bedroom. Rosamund hesitated, then pushed open the door. Emily had flung herself down on the rug beside the bed. Her head was buried in her arms, and she was sobbing with fury and distress.

"You don't trust me. I promised, and you still don't trust me."

"I do trust you," insisted Rosamund. She knelt beside her sister, trying to find the right words to explain. "Emmie, I understand why you feel like this, but it's not what you think. I'm not trying to rip you off. I'm doing this because I want to keep you safe."

"And you expect me to let you go alone?"

"I won't be alone. I'll have Gibraltar to help me."

"You'd rather be with him than me."

"That's not true."

"Yes, it is. Do you think I'm stupid?" Emily looked up, her eyes streaming. "You can't leave me behind. We belong with each other. I *can't* be the only Miniver. If we get caught, we *must* be caught together."

"That's rubbish, Emily," Rosamund spoke sharply. "This plan might be our only hope, but I'd rather scrap the whole thing than risk both our necks. Besides, what about Papa King? What about Millamant? If Madame caught us, she'd have them both murdered before breakfast. Don't you have a responsibility to them?"

"Milly would want us to stay together."

"Milly would want you to be safe," said Rosamund remorselessly. "You know she always told us to look after each other, and that's exactly what I'm doing. Besides, there's something else you haven't thought of. Papa King wants me to be the next Queen of Artemisia. That makes you next in line if I get caught, but if something happens to both of us, Madame has won. She'll become queen, and there'll be no one left to stop her. You know that, Emmie. There isn't any choice."

Emily had run out of arguments. She still did not agree, but she knew that the fight was lost. "All right, Rose," she said. "If that's what you want me to do, I'll do it. Just promise me you'll come back. We've already been separated once. I couldn't bear it if it happened again."

11

THE HIDDEN PAST

Madame stood at her office window in the Artemisia Palace, looking out across Queen Rosamund Boulevard. A workman was standing on a ladder on the other side of the street, slowly stripping a giant image of Emily and Rosamund Miniver off a billboard. A piece of paper flapped in the middle of Rosamund's mouth, as though she had a missing tooth. *Delaney's of George Street*, read the slogan, *Where the Minivers Shop*.

"Not any more," said Madame. She pulled down the blind and returned with satisfaction to her desk. Its shabby surface was covered with the papers she was working on, among them a freshly faked copy of the Artemisia Top Ten showing the new unimproved version of "Miniver Morning" at Number One, and the latest report from Operation Miniver, telling her that there had been no overnight graffiti attacks by the Minivers Underground. Perhaps, thought Madame, this meant they had given up. She certainly hoped so.

Madame put the report into the filing tray and picked up an envelope marked *PERSONAL*. The handwriting looked familiar, and she ripped it open and scanned the letter inside. It took several seconds for her to grasp its meaning. Madame uttered a sharp cry of fury. How dare Livia think she could give up her search, without a word of explanation? Well, it wouldn't do. Livia *was* going to find the Most Secret Room, if Madame had to take her by the scruff of the neck and throw her down the basement stairs. Madame shoved back her chair. As she did, her second-hand desk, which was propped up by a telephone book, gave a wobbly lurch and deposited all her papers on the floor.

"Adelaide!" yelled Madame. "*Adelaide!*"

A secretary in a smart grey suit opened the door. "Yes, Madame?"

"Adelaide," said Madame, "I've decided this office is too small for me. Clear this mess up, and see that my papers are packed and taken down to the Walnut Office immediately."

Adelaide stared at her. "The Walnut Office?"

"You heard me," Madame snapped. "The Walnut Office. I don't imagine Papa King is going to use it again. You can clear all his things out while I'm meeting with Len later this morning."

"Very well, Madame." If Madame had been more

observant, she might have noticed an angry tinge come into Adelaide's cheeks. She had been Papa King's secretary for over twenty years, and had strong, if secret opinions about his daughter. "By the way, there is a young man here from the City Archives. I told him he couldn't see you without an appointment, but he wouldn't go away. He gave me this envelope. Would you like Security to have him removed?"

Madame was about to say yes, when some instinct made her pause. It was in the City Archives that Rosamund Miniver had once tried to hide. It was also the place where Livia worked, and where she had been searching for the Most Secret Room. At the thought of Livia, Madame's anger was tempered by a vague disquiet. There had to be a reason why Livia had become so defiant. . . Still struggling with this spider web of half-made connections, Madame changed her yes to a no, and held her hand out for Adelaide's envelope.

"The fellow who gave it to me is called Tom McMahon," said Adelaide. "He says he works for the City Archivist."

Madame had never heard of Tom McMahon. She shook the envelope's contents on to her desk. There were two grainy photographs of Titus, obviously taken by security cameras at the Archives, and a photocopy of an Archives stack slip with his name at the top. The files he had asked for were Department of Works employment records, from the time of old Queen Rosamund. What on earth could Titus want with those? Mystified, Madame flipped the photocopy over and found a note on the back from Tom McMahon, addressed to herself. Madame read it. Her complexion was naturally pale, but in that moment, it turned so white that even her freckles seemed to vanish.

"Send him in!" Madame cried, in a hoarse, panicky voice. "And get me Operation Miniver on the telephone! I want Ron Burton down here as quickly as possible. If Titus thinks he's going to get away with this, he's got another thing coming!"

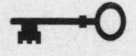

At six o'clock that evening, after a solitary meal of bacon, eggs and toast, Emily departed on operations. She was not looking forward to her job in what they now called the Control Van, but in the hours since her talk with Rosamund she had come to terms with what she had to do. Emily took with her the radio, a headset and Gibraltar's handwritten instructions. She left Rosamund still writing her speech on the lounge-room floor, screwing up page after page and tossing them over her shoulder. Emily knew Rosamund had never written anything before in her life. She could only hope, for all their sakes, that her sister would be able to pull it off.

Gibraltar wrapped Emily in a blanket, and she lay on the floor of Livia's car as he drove her to his caravan. It had been decided that to run the operation from Livia's house would be too risky, and that the van would be the next best choice. By the time Gibraltar and Emily arrived at the vacant allotment where the caravan was parked, it was just on dusk. Gibraltar turned into the broken-down driveway and bumped over the grass to park beside the van. As he killed the engine, the night air was filled with the sound of cicadas.

Gibraltar unlocked the van. He looked around carefully first, then whisked Emily straight inside.

"Goodness!" said Emily, as she pushed back the blanket. "What a lot of books!"

"Yes. There are, aren't there?" said Gibraltar. The lower of the van's two bunks and the whole of its tiny table were covered in books and papers. "You can have a look at them, if you like. Wait here, and I'll get the radio."

Emily climbed up on to the bench beside the table. The books were thick, and looked very serious, but her eye was caught by a picture on the jacket of one of them. It showed a portrait of a handsome middle-aged woman, and rather to her surprise Emily recognized it. She had seen the original many times in Papa King's study. The book was titled *Queen Rosamund of Artemisia: A Life*, and the author was Peter Barnabas, Gibraltar's real name.

"You wrote this!" said Emily, as Gibraltar came back into the van. "Queen Rosamund was Papa King's mother. Rosamund was named after her."

"That's right," said Gibraltar. "Fortunately, there's not much resemblance. Queen Rosamund was a rather frightening woman."

"I don't know much about her," admitted Emily. "Papa King was very fond of her, but I never heard him mention this book."

"Since he wasn't very happy with me for writing it, it's hardly surprising," said Gibraltar. "That's one of the few copies still around. Papa King had all the others confiscated and destroyed."

This was such a disturbing piece of information that it took Emily a few moments to process it. "Was that why Papa King sent you away?" she asked in a worried voice.

"No," said Gibraltar. "As a matter of fact, Papa King and I always got along very well. We disagreed about practically everything, but he once told me I was the only person he knew who was not afraid to tell him the truth. No. The reason he sent me away was because I helped saved his life."

"You saved Papa King's life?" exclaimed Emily. "How?"

"It was mostly Millamant's doing," said Gibraltar. "She found out there was a plot against him: I just took him the warning. You see, in those days Milly worked in the Archives as a cleaner. I was writing my book, and we knew each other well. One night, Milly saw Madame's mother, Susan, go into the Most Secret Room. She realized she was up to no good, so she locked her in and asked me to warn Papa King that something was afoot. That was how the whole plot came out. It turned out Susan had forged a will naming Madame as the next Queen of Artemisia and put it in the Most Secret Room. Madame was caught that same night, creeping into Papa King's bedroom when she thought he was asleep. She was trying to set fire to his bed."

"But – he's her father!" Emily stammered. "You really mean, Madame tried to burn her own father to death?"

"Why should it surprise you?" returned Gibraltar. "Madame has absolutely no conscience: you should know that by now. Of course, it was all kept secret. Papa King couldn't bear to have Madame publicly punished; for all her faults, he loved her very much. She and her mother were sent away, but all the details of what happened are stored in the Most Secret Room. That is why Madame is so desperate to find it."

Emily considered this. "Milly must know where it is," she said. "Did she ever tell you the secret?"

"No," said Gibraltar. "Papa King would have sworn her to silence and he trusted her. I was different. I knew too much, and so I was told to leave. Papa King was sorry about it. He even tried to give me money, but he would not change his mind."

"And now you're back." Emily looked up at Gibraltar, her expression puzzled. "There's one thing I don't understand. Rosamund and I are Papa King's foster daughters. If he treated you so badly, why are you helping us?"

"Because Milly wrote and asked me to," said Gibraltar. "And because I feel sorry for you. Papa King tried to turn you and Rosamund into some sort of ideal replacement daughters, but he never gave you the chance to be yourselves. I'd like to think, when all this is over, that you can stop being Minivers, and find out who you really are."

"Perhaps," said Emily sadly. She was sure Gibraltar was right, but finding out who you really were was no consolation for a girl who had thought she was famous, and found out instead that she was nobody at all.

It was eight o'clock, and Ron Burton was still at Operation Miniver Headquarters. Apart from the girl answering the Minivers Hotline, he was the only person in the building. All the security team was out, on Madame's instructions, scouring Artemisia for Titus. There was still no news, and Ron was just deciding he could not wait any longer, when the telephone rang.

Ron snatched it up. "Yes? What is it?" he said to Primrose, on the other end. "You missed him again? What on earth is he doing? That's the third Arnie Miller he's been to visit. This is getting crazy." He picked up a pencil and wrote some notes on a scribble pad in front of him. "OK. So Titus is obviously trying to find a particular person. No, I've no idea what he's trying to do. Madame didn't say. Just find out exactly how many Arnie Millers there are in Artemisia and send a team to all their houses. Report back to me when you've done that. Anything else you can tell me?"

"They're all old men," said Primrose. "One was eighty-three, and the other was ninety. The third one wasn't home. He was carted off to hospital last week with a broken hip. Speaking of hospitals, how's Alex?"

Ron looked at his watch. "He's due out of the operating theatre any time now," he said. "I must go to the hospital. Sandra will be waiting for me. Keep up the search, Primrose. I'm leaving you in charge for the next two hours."

With a nod to the girl on the switchboard, Ron grabbed his keys and hurried out to his car. It was only a short drive to the hospital, and though Madame would be angry when she found out he had left Primrose in charge of the operation, Ron did not care. He parked and ran up the hospital steps. A sign pointed him in the right direction, and he headed towards the lifts. The hospital foyer was full of people, and a fair head was bobbing along among the crowd in front of him. Ron looked at it blankly a moment, then suddenly started pushing his way towards it.

Titus was not aware that he had been seen, but he was moving quickly, and reached the elevator lobby before Ron did. He followed a nurse into a crowded lift. The doors closed in Ron's face and it started heading upwards. Ron shoved a couple of people out of his way and ran for the stairs. He was very fit, but the lift was a fast one and he had no way of telling where it was stopping. On the fifth floor he saw the nurse who had got into the lift before Titus.

"The man with fair hair – the one who got into the lift

with you – where did he get off? Quick, it's important. Operation Miniver." Ron flashed his pass and the woman's expression changed.

"Downstairs, two floors down – tell me, have you found Emily and Rosamund yet?" the nurse called after Ron, but he was already running for the stairs. He took them two at a time, bumping into a pair of doctors coming up and not even stopping to apologize. He emerged on a floor labelled Ortho-paedics, and suddenly something Primrose had said flashed into his head. Panting, Ron ran over to the nurse's station.

"Do you have a patient here called Arnie Miller?"

The nurse consulted a chart. "Ward 2A," she said. "Bed Sixteen. You can't go in though, he's got another visitor. His son's just arrived—"

Ron took his pass from his pocket and flashed it at her. "Call hospital security," he said. "If Arnie Miller's son's got fair hair and is wearing black jeans, there are people who want to speak to him very badly. Including me."

The curtains around Arnie Miller's bed were drawn when Titus entered the ward. He could see a nurse's feet moving around under its cotton edge and hear hushed conversation as she spoke to the patient. Three people were lying in the other beds, a man with a broken leg, and two ancient women. There was a smell of sickness and disinfectant.

The nurse emerged from behind the curtain. "You can go in," she said. "Don't be surprised if he doesn't know you, though. He's very muddled." She held back the curtain and Titus slipped around it. "Arnie? Your son Titus is here to see you."

Titus stepped forward. A very old man was lying in a bed with an oxygen mask on his face. His breathing was shallow and his skin was yellowish. When the nurse spoke, his eyes flickered open. They fixed on Titus, looking confused and puzzled, and then they closed again, with a slight shake of his head.

"Don't be upset," said the nurse. "He's got pneumonia and the oxygen isn't getting through to his brain. He's very weak, but he can tell you're there."

Titus nodded. He sat down on a plastic chair beside the bed and the nurse withdrew. Titus leaned forward, close to Arnie Miller's ear, and began to speak. He spoke for some time in a low voice and after a minute or so, the old man said something back. Titus listened intently. It was hard to make out exactly what the dying man was saying, but as he listened, his pale face settled into an expression of triumph. There would be no more guessing now about the location of the Most Secret Room. Madame could do her worst.

He *knew*.

12

RADIO FREE MINIVERS

"This is 98.5FM, Radio Artemisia, and you've been listening to 'Stop the Noise', the great single from new band Brain Dead. Coming up, we have the latest from Goth girl, Tracy T, a song from Venom, and an oldie but goodie from the Toe Rags. And remember, Radio Artemisia is guaranteed One Hundred Per Cent Minivers-Free Listening. Crazy Caro with you until 4 a.m. Venom now, with their new song, 'Don't Bite'."

The wail of guitars filled the glass booth where Caroline Melville was working the late shift. Caroline was very proud of her job as Radio Artemisia's newest DJ. It was true she sometimes felt like a vampire, working at night and sleeping during the day, but her career had to start somewhere. One day, Caroline intended to be a breakfast announcer and crack jokes with Tony de Burgh, Radio Artemisia's star DJ. It was Tony de Burgh who had come up with the idea of a Minivers-Free Radio Station, and Tony who had first played the eight-year-old Rosamund Miniver's terrible undubbed version of "Miniver Morning".

Caroline secretly liked the Miniver sisters' music. She knew perfectly well that lots of the other singers whose music Radio Artemisia played were just as over-dubbed as Rosamund, without the excuse of being eight years old. Just now though, it was not a good time to mention this. If bagging the Minivers was what it took to get her off the late shift and on to the breakfast show, then she had no choice but to say how much she hated every song they had ever made. Caroline had never been a girl to let the truth get in the way of what she wanted.

She cued up the next few tracks, took off her headphones and popped her head out into the main office. Simon, the station technician, was intent on the documentary he was piecing together for Tony. It was called *The Miniver Deception*, and it had to be ready for broadcast the following morning. Simon looked tired and ill-tempered, but Caroline knew he was always like this. She smiled brightly, and said, "Any chance of a cup of coffee?"

"I suppose I could put the jug on," Simon said in a grudging voice. "How do you like it?"

"White with two. Thanks." Caroline smiled again, for she believed being nice got you what you wanted. She handed Simon her empty coffee cup and he shambled off in the direction of the kitchen.

Simon flicked on the lights and filled the jug. He put the coffee in the cups and reached for the biscuit tin. It was unexpectedly light, and when Simon took off the lid, it was empty.

"What. . ." Simon peered into the tin, but there was not a crumb left inside. There had definitely been biscuits in there earlier, half a packet of orange creams, which were his favourites. Simon frowned. He knew that Caroline had not been out of her booth since her arrival, and Bruce, the security guard, was downstairs. But if neither of them had eaten the biscuits, where had they gone? At that moment, the jug boiled and a black-clad intruder slipped past the kitchen door and down the corridor. Simon was too busy making coffee to notice. It was only later that he realized the missing orange cream biscuits had been important after all.

Outside, behind the fence that ran along the back of the studio car park, a group of girls waited in a breathless huddle. They wore dark clothes, and their faces were blackened. Bridget and Carla were carrying a plastic crate labelled AAF. Fiona wore a backpack filled with Minivers CDs, and Mo had a rope slung over her shoulder.

"Tania's taking an awfully long time in there," Fiona whispered.

"I knew letting her go first was a dumb idea," said Carla. "You should have let me set the place on fire, the way I wanted to."

"And bring in the fire brigade? Don't be an idiot," said Bridget. "We're trying to help Rosamund and Emily, not get ourselves caught."

"All the same," said Carla wistfully, "it would be much more exciting than waiting about like this."

As she spoke, there was a soft footfall, and a slim dark shape slithered through a gap in the fence. The gang sprang to attention. Tania plopped down breathlessly on the ground and tossed a bunch of keys at Fiona.

"Got them."

"Tania! You found the keys!" exclaimed Fiona delightedly. She looked at the tag, but it was too dark to read it. "Are you sure they're the right ones?"

"Of course," said Tania, shoving the last of an orange cream biscuit into her mouth. "I got them out of the top drawer of the station manager's desk; it was dead easy. The best news is, there's hardly anybody in the building.

Just an announcer and one guy upstairs, and a security guard downstairs in the reception."

"The guard's the one who's mostly likely to cause trouble. We'll deal with him first," decided Bridget. She held her hand out for the keys. "We'll go in through the back door. Tania, what's the best place for an ambush?"

"CD library, I'd reckon," said Tania. "I couldn't see a phone in there, and the window's very small. I'll lure the guard inside, and you can lock him in. Come on. I'll show you where it is."

One by one, the girls slid through the gap in the fence. They found themselves in a dingy yard at the back of the radio station. A single light burned in one of the upstairs windows, but the building looked otherwise deserted. Like a line of ants, the attack force scurried across the asphalt to the back door. While the others crouched behind an industrial bin, Bridget quietly opened it with the key.

"Tania, you come with me," she whispered. "The rest of you, wait outside."

Tania and Bridget disappeared inside the building. Behind the bin, Fiona clicked on her radio and spoke swiftly and softly into the transmitter.

"B-Team calling Control Van. B-Team calling Control Van. This is Fiona. Over."

There was a pause, and then Emily's small voice

sounded briskly in her ear. "Control Van here, B-Team. State your position. Over."

"We're outside Target One. Bridget and Tania are securing the ground floor. Any word from G-Team? Over."

"G-Team has arrived safely at Target Two. No news yet. Report when you're all inside. Over."

"Roger, Control Van. Over and out."

Fiona snapped off the radio. The door opened and Bridget reappeared. At the same time, Tania oozed like a shadow from a high narrow window, and somersaulted lightly down into the car park.

"We got him!"

Somewhere inside the building, a male voice was yelling for help. Bridget beckoned the others hastily through the door. They hurried down a corridor, past the CD library, where the imprisoned Bruce was kicking at the door. His shouts had evidently been heard, for as the attack team reached the flight of stairs at the end of the passage, a second person called out from the landing. Immediately the girls moved into position, Mo and Carla on either side of the stairs.

"Bruce? Is everything OK?" The voice sounded like a young man's. As he ran down the last few, darkened steps, Mo and Carla jerked up their rope across the foot of the stairs. The newcomer tripped and went sprawling. Tania jumped on him. She dragged a sack over his head, and instants later, he was trussed up like a chicken ready for roasting.

"Mo. Stay here and guard the prisoners. The rest of you, follow me." Bridget jerked her head, and Fiona, Carla and Tania ran after her up the stairs. At the very top, they almost bumped into Caroline, who had come to see what was happening to Simon and Bruce. At the sight of the four desperate figures in black, she gave a terrified scream and fainted.

"This is really too easy," said Bridget. She leaned over the railing and called down to Mo, who was waiting below. "Hey, Mo – we've got another prisoner. Come and tie her up, would you? Any idea where we go now?"

"It's this way," said Tania. She hurried through the main office to the DJ's booth. Music was playing on the overhead speakers and Caroline's cans lay abandoned on the sound desk. Fiona took off her backpack and slung it to Tania. Carla was already putting on the headphones and tapping at the announcer's microphone.

"Let's get rid of this rubbish," said Carla. She pushed the Eject button on the Toe Rags and tossed the disc over her shoulder. Tania handed her a CD from Fiona's backpack and Carla looked at it in satisfaction. "*Miniver*

Dreaming – my favourite," she said and, slotting it into the machine, she started talking rapidly into the microphone.

"Sorry for that break in transmission. You're now listening to Radio Free Minivers! That's right, not Minivers Free Radio, but Radio Free Minivers, the station that wants to see the Minivers set free. Stay tuned for non-stop Minivers songs, and coming up, a special broadcast from our mystery guest. She'll be arriving at the studio shortly. Right now, here's Emily Miniver with her first solo hit, 'I want to be a star'. Hope you're listening, Emily. From your friendly DJs, Carla and Tania, and all at Radio Free Minivers – Minivers Forever! We love you!"

The sound of Emily's thin, pure voice poured out of the wall speaker. Fiona heaved a sigh of relief. She left the new DJs to their announcing and went back into the main office. Caroline was now lying on a sofa, tied up and gagged, but still unconscious. Mo and Bridget had dragged the unpleasant Simon up the stairs and were lashing him to a chair.

"Radio Free Minivers?" he sneered. "Oh, please. Spare me. What sort of kooks are you?"

Bridget loomed menacingly over him. "Shut up, weed," she said. "We need your help, and you'd better cooperate. A transmission's coming in soon from the studio at Miniver House, and we need you to patch it through to the broadcast frequency."

"Me?" said Simon. "No way! I'm not helping the Minivers. I hate them. Mingy little maggots. Let 'em rot, that's what I say."

"My mum and I are founding members of the Minivers Fan Club," said Fiona, furiously. "You'd better watch what you say, or you'll be sorry!"

"Oh, yeah? What are you going to do to me?" jeered Simon. "Call me a weed? Go and eat some spinach and come back when you've grown muscles."

"He thinks we're not serious, Fiona," Bridget remarked. "Well, he'll learn. Go and stand by that stereo. Take these earphones and plug them in, that's right. Simon," she went on, turning to him, "I see from your T-shirt that you're a Tracy T fan."

"I might be," said Simon sullenly. "She's better than the Minivers, that's for sure. She's a real woman, Tracy. And her band's awesome."

"Oh, yes. The Vampire Girls," said Bridget, with a faint sneer in her voice. "In that case, I can see why you're not so keen on our non-stop Minivers Marathon. Pop the earphones on him, Fiona. That's right. Now turn it up a bit, so he can hear our broadcast better."

Simon turned a little pale. "You don't have to, really."

"I think we do," said Bridget. "Can't quite hear that,

Fiona. Think I must be going deaf. And a bit more. . . What's that song? Isn't it 'Misty-Eyed Miniver'? Ah, that's better. Can you hear that, Simon? Fiona, can we go a bit further? I don't think Simon can hear."

"*No!*" Simon shook his head and writhed in the chair. "Stop! Stop, it's *awful*!"

"I think it's marvellous," said Fiona warmly. "I wish we had a stereo like this at home. It can go up three more notches, Bridget; do you want me to make it louder?"

"No, stop!" yelled Simon. "I'll do whatever you want. The transmission – when's it coming through? Just let me know and I'll do it for you, only please, turn that hideous noise off!"

"Turn it down, Fiona," said Bridget. "And get on the radio to the Control Van. As soon as Rosamund's in position, we're ready to move."

Papa King's office was on the first floor of the Artemisia Palace, in the private wing where its owner now lived in the twilight world of the very ill. It was a handsome room, with rich carpet, walnut panelling, and windows that opened on to a hidden courtyard filled with gardenias and white roses. The heady scent of the flowers floated up from the garden, but there was, nevertheless, something cold and unlived in about the room's grandeur. The Walnut Office had been abandoned since Papa King had suffered his stroke. Though it was regularly cleaned and dusted, nothing could make it look as if its owner was coming back.

Madame stood behind the desk, her hand on the leather chair back. A strange mixture of emotions ran through her shrivelled heart. Part of her felt satisfaction, a sense of unpleasant righteous triumph, that she could now move in here without anyone uttering a protest. Fighting against this, however, was a disagreeable memory of the last time she had stood in this very room. She had been on the other side of the desk, then, and her father had been sitting in the chair on which her hand now rested. It had been a short, but deeply humiliating interview. Madame could not forget how frightened she had felt throughout it.

"You really are a contemptible creature," Papa King had said. "I can hardly believe you're my daughter. Is this really the best you can manage?" He picked up the forged will, which Madame's mother Susan had tried to put in the Most Secret Room. Madame had said nothing. She had been terrified that Papa King would order her death, under secret orders. It was what his mother, Queen Rosamund would have done, she knew. Instead,

Papa King had told her to leave. "I never want to see you again," he said, as she left the room. "Make sure, Karen, that I don't."

Tears of rage and mortification sprang to Madame's eyes. Forgetting that there had once been tears in Papa King's eyes, too, she yanked back the leather chair and sat down at the desk. To the right of the pen tray was a photo of Rosamund and Emily Miniver in a silver frame. Madame snarled and swept it violently on to the floor.

There was a soft tap on the door. Madame hastily composed her face into a more queen-like expression and called out to Adelaide to come in. The secretary's eyebrows lifted at the sight of the broken photo frame, but she made no comment.

"Madame? Ron Burton's here with the prisoner."

"Send them in."

Adelaide opened the office door wide. Ron entered, accompanied by two other security guards. The three men were literally dragging the most filthy, abject figure Madame had ever seen. It was wearing what looked like dark jeans and a black T-shirt, but the shirt had lost a sleeve, and the person inside it was wet and slimy with filth. Madame wrinkled her nose. Ron and the guards did not look particularly clean either, and one guard had a bloody nose. There had obviously been a fight.

Madame looked her prisoner over. She felt savagely pleased, and a little excited. She was very glad indeed that Ron had not been gentle.

"What happened?" she asked severely. "He stinks. Where did you find him?"

"Culvert. Behind the Royal Artemisia Hospital. He fell in while we were chasing him. Almost got away." Ron spoke in snatches: it had evidently been an effort to get the prisoner up the stairs. He let go of his arm. Titus sagged and went down on one knee, breathing heavily.

"The hospital?" Madame stood up behind the desk and, unconsciously copying Adelaide, walked carefully over to Titus. His hair was gummed to his head with mud, he had a black eye, and a split lip that was so swollen and bloody that Madame could not help wondering whether he had lost a tooth. *Serve him right*, she thought, her fear of that morning giving way to indignation. *Serve him right.*

"You can leave now," she said to the other security guards. At a nod from Ron, they dropped Titus on the carpet and departed. Doing her best not to wobble on her unaccustomed high heels, Madame crouched disdainfully beside him.

"Well. Look at you," she said. "Mr Clever, himself. Only you were rather too clever, weren't you, Titus? You thought I didn't know what you were up to. You thought I was stupid. Well, the tables are turned now, aren't they? I've been one step ahead of you all the way, you filthy *traitor*." She spat the word right in his ear, but Titus neither recoiled, nor gave any sign of even hearing. Madame had been ignored for too much of her life to put up with such behaviour now. She grabbed hold of Titus's collar, and for a moment it looked as if she wanted to hit him.

"Don't ignore me like that," she hissed. "You're nothing, do you hear me? Until I scooped you up, you were scum in the gutter. You listen to what I'm saying—"

"*No. You listen to me.*" Suddenly, with one swift fluid movement that sent Madame flying backwards, Titus rose to his feet. His face was terrifying, and Madame gave a squeak. Ron took a hasty step forward and made as if grab Titus in a headlock, but the prisoner rounded on him so swiftly that Ron, too, could not help stepping back. It had taken three men to overpower Titus in the hospital culvert. Even in his injured state, Ron did not want to take him on alone.

"Coward!" shouted Madame. "Guards! Help me! Help me!" She scrambled to her feet and ran behind the desk. Titus followed and Madame shrieked. She snatched a lamp off a side-table and struck out wildly, but Titus dodged the blow calmly and grabbed the lamp from her hand. As he did, a small object on a chain swung out from under the neck of his T-shirt. Madame screamed.

"The key! He's got the key!"

"Yes. I have, haven't I?" said Titus. "Do you want to have a closer look?"

"Stop him!" yelled Madame.

Titus rounded on Ron. "Lay a finger on me," he said menacingly, "and you'll never find out where the Most Secret Room is." He waited for his words to sink in, then turned to Madame. "Now," he said. "Sit down, and do exactly as you're told."

13

ROSAMUND TRIUMPHANT

The Artemisia Royal Palace was surrounded by elegant gardens and fenced off from the public by a thick hedge and wrought-iron gates. Behind it, about five minutes' walk from the main building, was Miniver House. Most visitors thought the Minivers' old home was like something out of a fairy tale. It was a long low building with turrets at the corners like a castle, and it was painted the prettiest shade of pale pink imaginable. Inside, the fittings and furniture were exactly the right size for its tiny owners. For most of Rosamund's life, and all of Emily's, Miniver House had been a haven of peace and comfort. Now, it looked like something out of a nightmare.

Gibraltar and Rosamund crouched in the shadow of the big murraya hedge, staring across the lawn at the floodlit front of the house. Since Miniver House had been taken over by Operation Miniver, security had been tight. Only a few weeks before, Emily had been chased through the grounds by Ron's guards and nearly caught. Tonight, though, things were different. The guards who should have been patrolling the property were gone, and the whole place had an eerie deserted air. Even the sentry box at the main gate was empty, with nothing but a lowered boom gate to stop intruders. Ever since she had been kidnapped, Rosamund had been longing to go back home. In her wildest dreams, she had never expected it would be like this.

Gibraltar's dark eyes fixed watchfully on the floodlit terrace. "Something's wrong," he muttered. "Where is everybody? Even at this time of night, there should be some guards on duty."

"Do you think it's a trap?" Rosamund whispered.

"It might be. But how would the people inside know to expect us?"

Emily's voice sounded softly on the radio receiver in Gibraltar's ear. "Control Van to G-Team. Control Van to G-Team. B-Team has safely attained its target and begun transmission. Report your status. Over."

"What do we do now?" asked Rosamund. "We can't pull out, it's too late."

"If anyone's watching, they'll see us the moment we set foot on that terrace," said Gibraltar. "But people rarely challenge someone who's acting confidently. I think we should just walk up to the house, and if we're seen, we'll have to brazen it out." He touched the transmit button on his headset. "Emily? Are you listening? We're going in; over and out."

Gibraltar slung down his backpack and unzipped it. Rosamund stepped inside and crouched down, for once not grumbling about being shut up in the dark. She was genuinely too frightened, and as Gibraltar set out across the grass, she cringed in the bottom of the bag, and tried not to feel as if she was going to be sick. Bump, bump, bump. The backpack banged against Gibraltar's back as he walked purposefully over the lawn. Oh, why wasn't he going faster? Rosamund put her hand into her pocket and felt her speech, folded up and ready to deliver when they reached the studio. *If* they reached the studio. She began to sweat, as though the terrace floodlights were shining right inside the backpack and giving her presence away.

Gibraltar went up a couple of steps. There was a slight pause, and Rosamund heard the crack of breaking wood as he jemmied open a door. The backpack was quickly swung down, and a moment later she scrambled out into a familiar hallway, the one which led from the side entrance of Miniver House.

"We're in!" Rosamund whispered incredulously. "I didn't think we'd make it."

"No one even tried to stop me," said Gibraltar. "But I'll have been recorded on the security cameras, so we mustn't waste any time. Come on." Beckoning her on with his jemmy, he padded down the hall. It led to the main entrance, and on the way they had to pass by a normal-sized doorway. It was the conference room, where Rosamund and Emily had once met the press, and given parties for other celebrities. Its door was ajar, and when Rosamund peeped around it she saw the room beyond was full of office furniture and desks, all empty. A lonely girl sat at a switchboard, reading a novel. She was wearing a pair of headphones, which had evidently muffled the sound of their arrival.

Gibraltar put his finger to his lips and drew Rosamund swiftly away.

"What's she doing?" Rosamund hissed.

"Answering the Minivers' Hotline, of course. Didn't you see the sign?" He pointed. Sure enough, a laminated sign on the door read *Operation Miniver*. It was too far above Rosamund's eye level for her to have noticed.

"*That* is Operation Miniver? I thought it was meant to be huge!" Rosamund was incredulous. "Where is everybody?"

"Apparently not here. Come on. We must get to the studio, quickly, before anyone sees us."

They hurried on through another door, this time Miniver-sized, so that Gibraltar had to stoop. It led to the front hall, where a flight of polished stairs swept up to the floor above. Rosamund stopped. Her broadcast, and everything else they were here to do, was forgotten in the shock of the ruin in front of her. The barbed wire and floodlights in the garden had not lied. Miniver House looked like it had been through a war.

"What have they *done*?" she exclaimed in a stifled whisper. The lights were switched off, but the outside floodlights cast a moon-like glow over the wreckage of her beautiful home. "Where are my pictures – and all the furniture? Everything's gone. Someone's stolen it!" Her thoughts were flooded by a terrible vision of Madame, holding a giant garage sale of miniature belongings. It was so clear that for a moment, Rosamund was unable to stir. Then Gibraltar was urging her up the stairs, his long legs taking the tiny steps three at a time, and Rosamund reluctantly followed him, trying not to see the torn wallpaper, the dirt and rubbish, and the filthy slogans painted on the walls outside what had once been her bedroom. At the foot of the turret stairs, she trod on something hard and heard it snap under her foot. It was a gold CD, ripped out of its frame, and thrown like an abandoned frisbee on to the floor.

If Artemisia was ever ruled by Madame, thought Rosamund, *the whole city would soon look just like Miniver House*. As she followed Gibraltar up the turret stairs, a dreadful possibility struck her for the first time. Their whole plan depended on the studio being in a usable condition, but what if it, too, had been ransacked? The equipment it contained was valuable and it would be just like Madame to steal it. When they reached the top of the spiral staircase, however, the studio door was safely locked. Someone had pinned another notice above the doorknob. It read:

OPERATION MINIVER

RESERVED FOR PRIVATE USE
DO NOT ENTER

"That's interesting," said Gibraltar and quickly forced the lock. Rosamund followed him into the room. She saw immediately that her fears were unfounded, for the studio was almost exactly as she and Emily had left it. No one had stolen the equipment: in fact, it was clearly in use. Great loops of tape hung over the backs of the chairs, and there was an empty coffee cup and several CD singles on the table next to the sound desk.

Rosamund picked one up and dropped it instantly, as if she'd been burned. It was "Miniver Morning: Unmasked". Someone had used their very own studio to make a mockery of her and Emily, and from the look of the work in progress, there was more of the same to come.

"Leave that!" ordered Gibraltar. He shut the door and bolted it, and Rosamund sat down, relieved after so long to be sitting in a chair the right size for her. She heard Gibraltar talking rapidly on the radio to Emily, telling her that they were in position and ready to go. Rosamund put her hand into her pocket for her speech. A sick feeling rose suddenly in the back of her throat. She felt again, then jumped off the chair and started rattling through Gibraltar's backpack.

"Gibraltar. My speech – it's not here! I can't find it! It's gone!"

"What do you mean, Rose?" said Emily. "It can't have gone. You can't have lost it." She was sitting crouched over the radio on the caravan table. Until this moment, her job had been dull and seemingly pointless. Now Rosamund's voice came crackling almost hysterically over the air.

"I'm telling you, I don't have it. It was in my pocket on the way in, I remember checking it. I must have dropped it. Over."

"Can you go back and look for it? Over."

"Gibraltar's already doing that. Emily, I'm frightened. I don't know what to do!"

A red light flashed on the set. "Hold, please," said Emily to Rosamund. She flicked a switch and Bridget's voice came through on another frequency.

"B-Team to Control Van. Our technician is standing by. State your instructions. Over."

"One moment, please, B-Team." Emily paused, her hand still on the switch. She closed her eyes, remembering the many times she had played out this scene in dressing rooms at concerts and television studios, when her sister had succumbed to stage fright and declared she could not go on. Yet every time, at the last moment, Rosamund had lifted her chin and walked out on to the stage, and nobody in the audience had ever known. Emily drew a deep breath and threw the switch back to Miniver House.

"Rose, that was Bridget. They're waiting for you at Radio Artemisia. You've done this a hundred times before. It's no different to any other broadcast. Just think of your fans and you'll remember what to say. Over."

"It's not the same. They're not fans any more, why should they want to listen to me? Over."

"Because Minivers are for people to love," said Emily, desperately. She knew she was clutching at straws but she could not think of anything else to say. "You know that, Rose. Over."

"That's not true, Emmie. It never was true. I'm not a fool. Stop pretending; you don't believe that any more than I do."

The red light came on again, flashing urgently. "Wait, Rose," said Emily. A deafening noise rattled her ear drums as she switched to Bridget and she threw up her hands to clutch her headphones. "Bridget, what's that noise? It sounds like an explosion. Over."

"It was an explosion, Control Van. I think we've got company." Bridget's voice was matter of fact. "Better be quick. We're in position and the building's in lockdown, but I can't say how long we can hold. Over."

"Wait for instructions, B-Team. Over and out." With trembling fingers, Emily flicked the radio back to Rosamund's frequency. "Rose, you've got to do it without your notes. They're under attack at the station. If you don't speak in the next couple of minutes, you'll miss your chance. Over."

"I can't!" Rosamund's voice sounded in panic. "I can't do it, Emmie. It's not just over. It's *over*."

At Radio Artemisia, everything was confusion. Mo and Bridget were pushing chairs, desks and bookcases across doors and windows, barricading themselves inside as best they could. Fiona had taken Carla's place inside the DJ's booth, and Tania was urging Simon to hurry up and make the connection to Miniver House. Carla was on the roof. She had climbed out through a manhole, and was hurling home-made smoke bombs down into the car parks. The bombs were harmless, but the smoke they let off was black and choking. Carla had made them for her forthcoming revolution back at Delinquent Central. She had decided to donate them to the Minivers' cause.

Fiona looked out the window at the security guards gathering in front of the building. The smoke was making it impossible for them to reach the doors, and several were conferring by the studio gates. "They can't get in," she reported. "Carla's smoke's forcing them back!"

"Not for long, it won't," said Simon, from the sound desk. "They'll bring in gas masks any moment now. You'll see."

"Shut up, you." Fiona punched repeatedly at the transmit button on her radio, but though the light went on, Emily did not seem to be answering. Tania shoved another Minivers CD into the player. Her face was white, and her voice was wobbly as she made the announcement.

"Stay tuned, Minivers fans. Our special guest will be arriving at the studio any moment. Meanwhile, here's another great Minivers song, 'Small Heroes'. Keep listening!"

Simon sniggered under his headphones. Fiona wanted to slap him, but there was no point. Outside, the sound of police sirens rent the air. Fiona stole a glance out the window, saw the blue lights of the patrol cars and worse, a fire engine, backing into the narrow courtyard at the front of the building. Its ladder was slowly extending over the building. *Come on, Rosamund*, she thought. *Emily, why aren't you answering? We don't have time for this, come on!*

"Too late now," said Simon nastily. He too, had seen the fire ladder. Fiona's radio receiver suddenly crackled next to her ear. A calm voice spoke.

"Control Van to B-Team. Rosamund is in position and waiting. Stand by to patch her in. Counting you in now, G-team. Five . . . four . . . three . . . two . . ."

"This is Rosamund Miniver."

In Gibraltar's van, Emily relaxed. She had switched

on her ordinary radio, and Rosamund's voice came through sounding confident and clear as she had known it would. At Radio Artemisia, Tania and Fiona clasped hands and listened. Mo and Bridget paused with their shoulders against a bookcase, while Carla's smoke bombs exploded outside.

In her car outside Miniver House, Livia, who had never believed they would pull this off, clutched the steering wheel, desperately willing it to be over. And in the palace, in the private wing where nobody now went but doctors and nurses, Papa King lay in his bed, surrounded by softly humming equipment. His night nurse had left the radio on while she had gone to make a phone call, and though he could not move a muscle, his old dark eyes were glistening with tears.

"This is Rosamund Miniver. I'm here tonight at Radio Free Minivers to tell you about the incredible things that have been happening to my sister Emily and me over the last few weeks. I don't have time to explain everything, but the Minivers have been in terrible danger. We've been kidnapped, chased, and in hiding. We've gone hungry, and had to sleep out in the open, in fear of our lives. Worst of all, some of our enemies are the very people we expected to protect us. But that's not what matters. What matters, is that I'm finally able to speak for Emily and myself.

"Many times over the last few weeks we've had to ask ourselves who we are. Personally, I always thought I knew the answer to that question. I was Rosamund Miniver and I was famous. It never occurred to me to wonder what I did to deserve all that attention. I sold lots of CDs. I could dance and sing. I had a beautiful house and masses of clothes, and more money than I really knew what to do with. I took it all for granted, because for a long time I believed that Minivers were for people to love. I now know that was wrong. The fact is, that what people loved was not the real Rosamund Miniver, but the version of me they saw on TV and read about in the news. That Rosamund was perfect. She never did anything wrong, or foolish. The fact is, of course, that I was never really like that. There were times when I was selfish and spoiled and didn't behave as well as I should have. I did things that affected other people because I just didn't think. Now some of those stories are being spread around by our enemies and people are starting to say that, instead of being all good, Emily and I must have been all bad. That's not true, either. I'm not trying to make excuses for our behaviour. I'm just trying to say that the truth lies somewhere in between, and that on behalf of both of us, I'm sorry for anything we've done that's hurt you.

"I know that many of you listening will now be wondering whether it's really me talking, or whether I'm some kind of impostor. Well, it is me, the real Rosamund Miniver, and though I'm tired and dirty and scared tonight, I'm here to tell you that Emily and I are not giving up. The rumours that we're dead are not true. What is true, though, is that the horrible stories you've been hearing have been spread to stop you helping us. I don't have much time left to talk, but I want you to know that if you care, there are some things you can do to help. First of all, don't ring the Minivers Crisis Line. Despite what they say, it's being run by our enemies, and any information you give them will be used to try and capture us. Second, don't pay attention to any news that comes out of the Minivers Fan Club. The club's behind all the anti-Miniver riots you've been seeing, and the committee's working for Madame. She might be Papa King's daughter, but Madame's not what she seems, either. Don't trust her! Listen to me now, and remember that the Minivers have always been Artemisia's friends. We might be in trouble, but we want you to know that as long as our fans stick by us, we'll get through this somehow. And that's a prom—"

Rosamund's voice stopped abruptly. Emily banged her radio, but there was nothing to hear but static. She grabbed the transmitter, but before she had a chance to say anything, a signal came through and she heard Fiona, gabbling in panic.

"They've stormed the station! They came in through the ceiling, they've got Carla and Bridget. Someone's hit Mo over the head, I think she's unconscious. Over!"

"Fiona! Fiona, you've got to hide! Get into a cupboard, anything, don't let them catch you! Over!" A terrible racket sounded in Emily's earpiece, as if someone was overturning furniture, and there were shouted orders and Tania's voice in the background, clearly screaming, "Let me go, you—" The transmission stopped. Her hands shaking, Emily waited a few seconds, then switched to the other frequency.

"Control Van to G-Team. Control-Van to G-Team, we've got an emergency –"

Emily broke off. She had been so busy coordinating the others that she had almost forgotten about herself. Now she heard something that even the din coming over her headphones could not drown out: the sound of a car reversing slowly towards her. There was a loud clunk, and the whole caravan shuddered around her. Emily grabbed the radio to stop it falling into her lap.

"Gibraltar – Gibraltar, can you hear me?" The line was dead. Emily ripped off her headpiece. She jumped off the bench and ran to the door, but it was locked or jammed and would not budge. The coupling at the front of the van dropped into place with a heavy thunk and Emily fell over on the floor. The car revved its engine. With a violent lurch and a squeak of rusted axles, the caravan jerked forward and rolled away.

14

THE AFTERMATH

In the Walnut Office, Madame, Ron and Titus sat through Rosamund's broadcast in silence. The emergency had caught them by surprise. Even Titus had not expected it, but he listened to Rosamund speaking with a curious, almost respectful expression. At eleven o'clock a call came through from Primrose, reporting in on the siege at the radio station. Ron spoke to her rapidly for several minutes, then put down the receiver.

"They've stormed the building. Primrose has sent three teams in through the roof. They've caught four of the culprits, but there's no sign of the Minivers."

"There won't be," said Titus. He was lounging in a velvet armchair with his legs, still in their filthy jeans, slung over the arm. "You can't expect to find them there. Everyone inside that radio station will be taken prisoner within the next five minutes. I don't think even Rosamund Miniver would be stupid enough to risk that."

"But Rosamund was there with them," said Ron. "We heard her speaking, and it sounded like a live broadcast. I know her voice. It was definitely her."

"That doesn't mean she was in the building," said Titus. "No. Rosamund will have made her speech from somewhere else, quite nearby. Somewhere she's familiar with, where she knows the equipment. A place you left unattended, while your men were chasing me all over the city."

"Miniver House?" said Ron.

"I'm surprised you needed to be told," said Titus. "Yes. Miniver House."

"But what should we do?" said Ron. He had quite forgotten the fight in the culvert, and had slipped naturally back into their old way of doing things. "The whole team's down at the radio station."

"We go down to Miniver House ourselves, of course," said Titus. "I'd say the two of us are more than a match for one Miniver, wouldn't you?" He turned to Madame, who was sitting, stiff and silent, behind Papa King's desk. "We'll be leaving you now, Karen. Don't worry, you're still going to be queen – on my terms – but just for the moment, Rosamund must come first. I hope you'll understand." Titus stood up and smiled. "By the way, I'm not a greedy man. You can keep the office – and the desk."

He limped out of the room with Ron.

Madame waited until their footsteps had faded along the passage, then slammed her fists down on the desktop with a hoarse cry. The rage she had been too frightened to express when Titus had been in the room erupted inside her. Everything had gone wrong. For months, Titus had been pretending he was helping her, yet all the time he had been working behind her back, first, stealing the key, then finding the Most Secret Room, and now, which was almost worst of all, capturing Rosamund Miniver. Madame's heart, never very large, contracted with a hot and violent hatred at the thought. She wanted to kill Titus. She wanted to destroy him utterly, to grind him to tiny pieces under the heel of her shoe. Yet what could she do? The moment she even tried to stop him, Titus would release her secret to the world, and she would be revealed as a would-be murderer who had tried to steal her own father's throne.

It wasn't fair. It simply wasn't fair. To have come so close, after all those terrible years spent in exile, and then to have everything snatched away at the final moment! She would not be Titus's puppet. Hadn't she a right to the throne? Wasn't she Papa King's daughter? The old man was practically dead anyway; it was time Artemisia moved on. A grim picture of a future spent entirely at Titus's beck and call was swiftly followed by another realization, one that made Madame even angrier. None of this was her fault. It was Livia who was to blame for everything. If she had found the Most Secret Room when she had been told, instead of mooning about drawing, and painting their grandparents' house ridiculous colours, Madame would be safely on Papa King's throne by now. Furthermore, and this was something that made Madame particularly indignant, she was sure Livia had lied. That was a privilege Madame reserved for herself, and if Livia thought she was going to get away with it, she was wrong. Madame was on to her now, and whatever it took, she was going to make Livia pay.

Madame reached for a notepad and scrawled something angrily across it. She rang the buzzer for Adelaide and the secretary came into the office.

"Madame?"

"The security guards," said Madame. "Are they all down at the radio station?"

"Some have just come back, I think," said Adelaide. "I saw a car pull up five minutes ago."

Madame tore off the sheet of paper and handed it to her. "Go and find them," she ordered. "I want them to go to this address and burn it down."

Rosamund and Gibraltar ran across the Miniver House terrace. Floodlights streamed hotly down on them, and the unseen eyes of the security cameras followed their passage across the lawn. They reached the boom gate on the drive, ducked under it, and ran for the shrubbery. When Rosamund fell behind, Gibraltar reached down and swung her up on to his shoulder. She clung to his neck like a monkey and did not let go.

Rosamund could hardly believe they were getting away. When her broadcast had been cut off, she had expected every alarm in the house to go off, and hordes of security guards to appear from nowhere. Instead, it seemed as if their first impressions had been right. Miniver House really was deserted and though Rosamund was at a loss to explain why, there was no time to wonder. A few seconds later they reached the hedge and dived into its rustling, scratchy cover. Rosamund dropped to the ground and squeezed between the bars in the fence behind it, and Gibraltar quickly shinned up over it and vaulted down into the street. The car was waiting for them, just where it should be, with its engine running and Livia sitting behind the wheel.

The radio was on, but the broadcast had stopped and there was nothing to be heard on Radio Artemisia but static. Livia looked up as they jumped into the car and snapped on her indicator. The doors closed on

Rosamund and Gibraltar, and Livia pulled out from the kerb and drove away.

"Were you listening?" asked Rosamund breathlessly. "Did you hear my speech?"

"Yes, I did," said Livia. "I thought you did very well."

"They cut me off before I finished," said Rosamund. "I didn't get to talk to the audience, either."

"I don't think that matters," said Gibraltar, unhooking his headset from around his neck. "The important thing is that you made the broadcast. I'll contact Emily now, and tell her we're safely out."

Gibraltar turned off the car radio and put on his headset. He pushed the transmit button over his ear. "G-Team to Control Van. Come in, Emily. Over."

There was an answering hiss of white noise. Gibraltar waited a moment, then tried again. "G-Team to Control Van. Are you there, Emily? Respond, please. Over."

Rosamund leaned anxiously forward from the back seat.

"Let me try—"

"Gibraltar!" Emily's voice suddenly crackled into his ear. "Thank goodness you're there. I've been trying and trying to get through. Something terrible's happened. Someone's hitched a car to your van and driven off with it. I'm still inside, and I can't get out!" Her voice was loud enough for the others to hear. Livia swerved slightly. Rosamund jumped up into the space between the two front seats.

"Emily? Are you all right?"

"Rosamund, get down on the floor," snapped Gibraltar. "Someone will see you. Livia, drive around the corner. Emily. Do you know who's got you? Which direction are they heading? Over."

"I don't know!" Emily's voice sounded high and panicky. "It's an old blue car, that's all I can see. We're on the motorway, I think. Northbound. We're heading for the city. There's a hospital. A big one – the Royal Artemisia. And we've just passed a cemetery. We're going on to the bridge now. I can see the river. Over."

"Emily, listen to me. We're in Livia's car. We'll try and intercept you when you come off the bridge, but you must keep calm. Do you think you can get out of the van? Over."

"I've tried to get out already. I've done everything I can think of. The door's been jammed and the windows don't open wide enough. We're coming off the bridge. I can see the city. Where are you? Over."

"We're stopped at a light. . . Turning back into Miniver Boulevard. We're looking out for the van—"

"There it is!" shouted Livia, and Rosamund, against instructions, bobbed up again like a jack-in-the-box. "Hold on! I'll try and cut it off!"

She put her foot down on the accelerator and the car shot forward through the sparse late-night traffic. A shabby blue sedan was heading in the opposite direction, weighed down at the back by Gibraltar's van. It was travelling slowly, with its indicator on, as if the driver did not know where to turn. Livia's car bore down on it. The sedan began to turn across the traffic, into the main gates of the Artemisia Royal Palace. Livia gave a shout. She flattened her foot until her car almost flew, then jammed on the brake and slewed to a halt in front of the gates. There was a puff of smoke, a stink of burning rubber, and the sedan towing the caravan ploughed with a crash into the rear of Livia's car.

Rosamund was flung off the back seat, hitting her head with a resounding thump as she fell. She landed on the floor, half-stunned, and by the time she scrambled up, Gibraltar had flung open the door and was running towards the van. Rosamund stood up shakily on the seat, struggling to see exactly what was happening. The yellow car had stopped at a right angle to the road, its headlights shining through the iron gates into the palace car park. Rosamund heard Livia scream, and her dazed eyes snapped instantly into focus. Caught in the headlights, in the act of walking out the palace door, were Ron Burton and Titus.

For a moment the two men stood staring at them. They were dazzled by the headlights, and clearly thought they were looking at an ordinary traffic accident. Then Titus saw Gibraltar on the footpath. He gave a shout and started to run. Livia shoved her hand against the horn.

"Gibraltar! Gibraltar, come back!" She wrenched the steering wheel to the right and the yellow car began to move. There was a crunch of damaged metal as it pulled away from the blue sedan, and it began rolling forward, the open door flapping as it gathered speed. Rosamund grabbed at it, nearly falling out of the car. She heard Gibraltar's feet pounding back over the pavement, and then he jumped and landed on the front seat, slamming the door behind him just as Titus reached it.

Livia stamped her right foot on the accelerator. The yellow car skidded forward, bounced off the gutter, and roared through a red light on to the on-ramp leading to the bridge and southern motorway. Over her shoulder, Rosamund saw the caravan, with Emily inside it, disappearing into the palace courtyard.

"Emily! We've got to go back for her!"

"We can't," said Gibraltar. "They're already following us. Look." He pointed, and Rosamund saw a car's headlights turning out of the palace gates. Livia was watching too, in her rear-vision mirror. Her hands tightened on the steering wheel and she tried to accelerate, but her damaged car was already travelling as fast as she could make it go, and its engine whined in protest.

"What shall we do?" she cried. "They're catching us up. We'll never outrun them in this heap!"

"We'll be fine," said Gibraltar. "Just keep your cool, and do as I tell you. Stay in this lane and get ready to swerve on my count. One . . . two . . . three – off on to the bypass, quickly!"

Livia yanked down the wheel. Her car swerved across two lanes of traffic and shot on to an off-ramp, narrowly missing a lorry in the process. The lorry slammed on its brakes and the white security car carrying Ron and Titus along the motorway had to brake behind it.

Behind the wheel Ron yelled, and lost control of the car. There was a screech of tyres, a tremendous bang as they clipped the lorry, and then the whole car spun around in a darkened blur. A second later, it hit a metal barrier with a rending crash and all was still.

In the passenger seat, Titus was shaken, but unhurt. The roof was crushed. Broken glass was everywhere, and beside him, Ron lay slumped against the steering wheel. Blood streamed from a cut on his forehead, but he was still breathing, and Titus had no doubt he would survive. Meanwhile, the yellow car carrying Gibraltar and Rosamund Miniver had disappeared and Titus knew that for now he had lost them.

Titus took off his seat belt. He leaned over, pulled a notebook and pencil out of Ron's pocket, and carefully jotted down from memory the registration number of Livia's car. He did not know who she was, but it would be easy enough to find her. The Minivers might think they had eluded him, but they would not keep their freedom for very long.

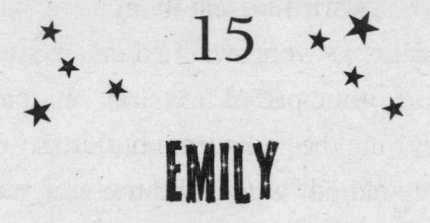

15

EMILY

Emily crouched on the caravan table, curled up in a tiny ball like a mouse. Her stomach was cramped and her mouth tasted of fear. She did not understand why the others had driven off. She only knew that she must face whatever was about to happen completely alone.

The caravan now stood in the courtyard between the palace offices and the private wing where Papa King actually lived. Emily had tried everything to get out. The door would not open, the windows were too thick to smash, and the radio had fallen on to the floor when the cars had crashed and was broken. Nothing had worked, and now she was trapped. Through the window Emily saw the square, shambling figure of her kidnapper, standing in the courtyard. He was dressed scruffily in baggy shorts and a khaki shirt, and wore a small towelling hat on his head. Emily did not know who he was or why he had captured her, but he seemed to be waiting for someone to come and take charge.

Five minutes went by, then ten, and then fifteen. It was dark outside, with no moon, and the lights inside the palace buildings were switched off. Emily grew sick with fear and anticipation. At last, a door opened unexpectedly in the adjacent building. A smartly dressed, grey-haired woman came out, and for a moment Emily allowed herself to hope. The elegant woman was Adelaide, Papa King's secretary, whom she had known since she was a baby. She tapped anxiously on the window and Adelaide glanced up. Their eyes met, and Adelaide looked away.

Upstairs in the Walnut Office, Madame was waiting for Adelaide to report. After what seemed a very long wait, the secretary came back, clicking down the polished corridor in her high-heeled shoes and letting herself in without knocking. She looked tired, and her mouth was a thin, grim line.

"I've spoken with him," she said. "It's true: he is Gibraltar's neighbour, and he does have one of the Minivers. He says he noticed someone inside the caravan and went to investigate. When he realized who was in it, he towed the caravan here."

"Did he say what his name was?" asked Madame.

"He's called Malcolm," said Adelaide. "He mumbled so much I couldn't make out his surname. He doesn't have any teeth."

Madame nodded. During her years in exile, she had made a number of rather disreputable acquaintances. Ever since her return to Artemisia, she had been afraid that one of these people would turn up and try to cadge off her. Fortunately, this toothless visitor did not sound like anyone she knew. She hoped he was not expecting her to buy him dentures.

"Why has he brought her here instead of Miniver House?" she asked.

"I gather," said Adelaide, "that he had trouble finding the right entrance. He was looking for Operation Miniver and he turned into the wrong driveway by mistake."

"Ah," said Madame. Her colourless eyes began to gleam. Perhaps, she thought, the situation was not as bad as she had feared. She would have to move quickly, though. There was no saying when Titus might be back.

"Make sure all the rooms overlooking that courtyard are emptied," she said to Adelaide. "We have to move fast now. Send two men down to secure the caravan and have the Miniver brought to my office."

"And Malcolm?" Adelaide coughed. "What should I do with him? I think he's expecting to get a reward."

"Get rid of him," said Madame. She was not going to waste any more precious money now. "Have Primrose see to it when she gets back. By the way, do you know which Miniver it is?"

Adelaide's grey eyes were sombre. "I'm not sure," she said. "But I think it's Emily."

The yellow car nosed out of the lane in which it had been lurking. Its headlights were off and thick black smoke floated out from under the bonnet. Livia put her foot down gingerly on the accelerator, and the car crept out into the street and drove away.

The engine made an ominous chopping noise. The black smoke grew thicker, and there was a tick-tick-tick, as if something loose was hitting the inside of the bonnet. The car crawled on to the main road and inched along the outside lane to the first exit. As they turned off and headed into the inner suburbs, Rosamund sat forward on the back seat.

"Where are you headed?"

"Home," said Livia. "Where else can I go?"

"But what about Emily?" exclaimed Rosamund. "We have to go back for her. She's still at the palace."

"Rosamund," said Gibraltar in a reasonable voice, "Livia's right. This car is about to break down. Emily has stopped answering the radio. We don't know what's happened to her. Until we find out more, we can't do anything to help her."

"We can't find out more if we don't go and look."

"We're not going to look," interrupted Livia. "This is it. It's over. I've done enough for you, Rosamund. I'm not going to risk everything I have, just because something's gone wrong with a plan I never wanted anything to do with in the first place."

"But you can't stop now." Rosamund's voice rose in a crescendo of panic. "Emily's a prisoner. They might kill her. She might be dead already, and it will be your fault!"

"Oh, shut up!" shouted Livia. "When are you going to learn this isn't just about Emily and you? What about the rest of us? What about me? What about Fiona and those other girls? Who do you think you are, Queen of Artemisia?" As she spoke, the engine gave a loud shudder, and died. The car puttered to a halt at the top of Daventry Street and Livia burst into tears.

Rosamund had opened her mouth to speak, but the hot words she had intended to say did not come out. She waited while Livia groped for a tissue, and said, quietly, "I'm sorry. I know you don't like me. I know it's not fair; you shouldn't have to help. But Emily is my sister. Just because you don't care, you can't expect me not to."

"I do care," said Livia. She mopped her face and blew her nose on the tissue. "You don't understand. It's because I cared that I helped you in the first place. But I can't go on. I have to stop now, or I don't know what will happen to me. I feel like my head is about to explode, like I'm going mad. I just can't do this any more."

"You don't have to," said Rosamund. "I know you never wanted to get involved. And you're right. I'm not the Queen of Artemisia, and I probably never will be. But if ever I get out of this mess, Livvy, I won't forget what you've done for me. I'll make it up to you. It might be goodbye, but it won't be goodbye for ever."

"I don't think it's goodbye at all, just yet," said Gibraltar quietly. He pointed down the street. Through a haze of drifting smoke, the orange glow of a fire could clearly be seen at the bottom of the hill. A smell of burning floated in through the car windows, not the oily stink of their overheated engine, but a wood fire smell, as if someone was having a barbecue and had put too much wood on the fire. In the distance they heard the sound of a fire engine. Livia and Rosamund sat staring at the blaze, unable, for a moment, to take it in.

"My house," Livia whispered. "Oh, no. My house."

Emily was dreaming of Papa King.

In her mind's eye she saw the courtyard as it had been on the day of her last visit. It was summer and the gardenia bushes were in blossom. The stone colonnades were bathed in sunshine, and the fountains played gently over the water lilies. She and Rosamund had been to afternoon tea with Papa King, and as they walked off together, arm in arm, on their way back to Miniver House, they looked up and saw him standing in the window of the Walnut Office. He was smiling, and they waved goodbye. He had blown them a kiss in reply, and it had been the last time he had ever done it, for that was the afternoon he had suffered his stroke.

There was a dull thump outside and the caravan door opened. Emily jerked upright, all thoughts of the past banished from her head. Two men came into the van, and in a last desperate effort she jumped off the table where she was sitting and charged their legs, hoping to make it to the door. She was not quick enough. As she dived for the opening, one of the men caught her by the scruff of the neck and tossed her painfully back into the van.

"Oh, no you don't." The man leaned over and hauled Emily off the floor. She bit and kicked, but they dragged her out into the courtyard. The kidnapper was no longer there. Everything was in darkness and though Emily's eyes darted wildly around the colonnades, she could see nowhere to run.

The men frogmarched her across the paving stones and into the palace. The red carpet and cream walls were exactly as they had been on that last day, and so were the carved wooden stairs at the end of the passage. Up, up, up, Emily was dragged, her tiny legs barely keeping pace with the men pulling her along. The struggle was tiring her, and she knew it was pointless, but she would not give in without a fight.

They reached the top of the stairs and turned into a passage. Emily knew it well, for it was the corridor that led to Papa King's private suite. Against all reason, her heart beat harder and she began to hope. They stopped at a door, the door of the Walnut Office, and when it opened, there was Adelaide in the outer office, just as she had been in the old days, when Papa King had stood at the window waving, and they had not known they were saying goodbye.

Adelaide hurried from behind her desk, her eyes averted. She opened the door into the main office, and for some reason, perhaps because they had reached their destination, or because they were simply tired of her struggling, Emily's captors loosened their grip. She slipped free and ran forward. The desk lamp was on and there was a figure in a dark suit bent over the desk. The sight was so familiar that, even as she realized it was impossible, Emily opened her mouth to say hello. Then the heavy door closed behind her and the figure put down its pen and looked up.

"Hello, Emily," said Madame.